STILLNESS ECHOES

A NOVEL

FRANK KINSLOW

Dedication

To my readers of many years — thank you for your dedication, support, and the great memories. This one is for you.

To my new readers — welcome aboard. I'm here for you.

To Paige — thanks mucho. Choo!

And to my wife, Martina — you still float my boat, darlin'. Here's to a lifetime of billowing white clouds, azure seas, and the wind at our backs. *Miluji Tĕ!*

CONTENTS

CHAPTER 1

The Box

She heard the metallic squeaking above and looked up. The blades of a single air vent high above rotated slowly, slicing shafts of sunlight, dropping them to the floor below. Eleonora was fascinated by the play of light and shadow, light then shadow. As she watched the light swallowed the darkness. Oneness. Stillness. The blade squeaked breaching the stillness.

The florescent light was flickering again — another reason not to be here after 6 p.m. That, and her migraines, which always began to gain momentum around this time. Flickering. She needed air.

She needed to get home to her tabby Socrates — the only creature who seemed to want her company without condition. The thought of his needy, nonchalant "I don't need you, but would love a good tummy rub" moods brought a weak smile. But she stayed. There was work to do.

She felt like a file clerk. She wasn't — not with two PhDs, 22 years in the field, and seven years at the museum. But she was being treated like one. She muttered as she moved down the dim hallway, fumbling for the switch. Finally, her hand found it. The fluorescents buzzed awake, scattering harsh, bluish light across row upon row of dusty, discolored file boxes. Eleonora always felt like holding her breath at first. The ancient mold. Tickled the throat.

This used to be her space. A sanctuary. A warm womb that once revealed the astonishing atrocities and triumphs of humanity. But as the cold light washed across her pallid face, she felt only the hollow ache of what she had lost.

Earlier that morning, Dr. Grubner had called her into his office. Grubner, who never missed an opportunity to remind anyone that he had once interned under a Nobel Laureate. Grubner, professionally entrenched and bitterly aware that his career had plateaued. He lifted himself up by belittling those beneath him — and Eleonora was an easy target.

She knocked quietly on his door — three times, the sound hollow to her own ear.

"Yes, yes, what is it now?" he barked.

"It's Eleonora, Dr. Grubner."

"Yes, I can see that. Take this file…" Tossed across the desk.

"What is…"

"Don't interrupt and you won't have to ask. The Late Antiquities file. Make sure it's on Whitehead's desk this morning. If he's decided to bring his head to work, he'll know what to do with it. Now stop wasting my time."

Years of smoldering resentment flared. Eleonora turned briskly on her heels and left without a word, shoulders hunched, neck cords taut. She stomped down the cold marble stairs. Catching her heel on the edge, her knee wrenched, and pain shot through her leg — sharp, searing, and familiar. An old injury. The Salona excavation. She grabbed the railing, her breath hissing between her teeth as she sank down to sit on the sweating stone step. The chill seeped into her, dulling the heat of her anger. Clutching the banister, she heaved herself up and tested her swollen knee. Good enough. She limped on.

Dr. Benjamin Whitehead sat at his desk, unaware of the storm of dark energy hobbling toward him. He heard her before he saw her. When she appeared, his smile shone instinctively — then faltered halfway, unsure if it had met friend or foe.

"Ellie! Are you all right?"

Her eyes mere slits.

"Dr. Whitehead, I am absolutely fine!"

He didn't believe her. He had seen her upset before, though no one else seemed to notice. She was just Eleonora. A ghost among many museum ghosts. To the world, she was dull gray. Uninspired. But Ben knew better.

"Dr. Whitehead, I…" she began.

He interrupted gently, "Please, Ellie. Call me Ben. Please."

"Dr. Whitehead," she repeated, hard as hurt. "I will not be able to retrieve your file from the archives until later this afternoon. I have my own—"

"What file?" Ben interrupted.

She exhaled sharply. "File No. 47-B from the Late Antiquities Scroll Collection."

"I don't know what you mean," he stammered. "That's a file I need — but how do you even know about it?"

"Grubner told me to find it and deliver it to you. He said, and I quote, 'Whitehead will tell you if he needs anything else."

Ben frowned. "Grubner was here first thing this morning. He asked what I was working on. I told him I was finishing the report today — as soon as I found the Scully File."

He shrugged. "Grubner said nothing more and just walked out. You weren't part of the conversation."

In seconds, Eleonora went from defensive, to confused, to quiet. Then she understood. She smiled.

"That makes sense," she said softly. "I should have expected that. I'm sorry."

The apology cracked something between them. Ben felt it. Eleonora had never offered him anger before — and now, an apology. Hopeful. A chance to

Ben leaned in. Cautiously, "You know you can count on me, Ellie. I'm here for you."

Startled at Ben's sincerity, she faltered. Caution. Doubt. Distrust. Fear. Old associates.

She stiffened. Petals closing before a unkind night.

Ben felt the shift. Resolved.

"Ellie?"

"Call me Eleonora," she said, and turned away.

Back at the archives Eleonora lifted her gaze to orient herself. She held the archival sleeve for Whitehead's file against her side as she serpentined through numberless stacked boxes.

She looked left, then right then to the far corner, dark and dank. There. Under a vulgar, red "EXIT" sign she found what she sought. A dusty, yellowing sign signifying section and row; Y-26.

Over the sign a rusty steam pipe hissed erratically through crumbled lagging. Eleonora imagined a tight-bunned school librarian shushing high-spirited middle schoolers. The image earned a brief smile. Short lived.

"Ah, of course at the other end of the archives." she mumbled. Eleonora started then stopped a piece of packing tape stuck to the heel of her shoe. She stepped on the tape with her other foot and scrapped it off on the rough cement. "What next?" She thought and began weaving her way through splintered palettes and misshapen boxes. The vulgar red exit sign her beacon.

She was almost there when her knee rebelled without remorse. It swelled. It throbbed. Her migraine throbbed in sympathy. She sat heavily on the nearest box to rest it. The aged wood bowed just a bit then held. Eleonora's ankle deeper purple. She was done. Emotions roiling. And now, the knee… betrayed.

She closed her eyes. She expelled a deep breath of desperation. Her breath went out… It did not go in.

Eleonora observed the interruption with quiet amusement. A single thought, "I'm not breathing." A second thought, "I don't need to breathe." A third thought never arrived. Eleonora was, in mind and body completely still.

Then, after a time a timid thought poked its way into her awareness. "Am I alive?" Nothing. Stillness. Again, "I must be alive. My mind is. Is my body?" Eleonora became aware of her body. She was overwhelmed. Her body seemed to encompass the whole universe, all of creation…and beyond. Beyond was nothing. Beyond was pure existence. Beyond was free. Eleonora was free.

Eleonora didn't know how long she sat on that ordinary yet momentous box. She did realize that it was the most momentous moment of her life. And she didn't know what to call it. How to describe it. What it had done to her. But most importantly she did not know how to get it back.

Elated but somewhat bewildered, Eleonora looked around the vast room. Everything remained where it had been, but nothing was the same. The stillness waited within her, was her. What was it waiting for?

Across the aisle, Eleonora's gaze fell on a timeworn wall clock, its hands frozen between moments. Its face lay dim beneath the high light, yet the brass rim caught the faintest gleam. The stillness waited within it! What was happening? Was she coming unglued? If so, it felt divine.

The same stillness was in both her and the clock. Put more accurately, both Eleonora and the clock were stillness. She didn't understand it. She knew it.

Somewhere, a thought, fragile as a butterfly's wing settled within. Latin, ancient — something she'd translated years ago:

Stilla et scies… Quod sum.

Be still, and you shall know… that I am.

They came, the words, then light as dandelion fuzz drifted away.

Be Still… and know.

And now she knew. Her essence, the essence of the box, the walls, the very blood now surging through her veins, Stillness.

Not "still" as in motionless. Still as in the origin of motion. Still as in the backdrop against which everything moves. Still like the movie screen upon which is cast the illusion of life.

She felt whole, peaceful at one with all things. The scientist eye could never accept the idea that we are all one. But now she knew it not through the scientist's laboratory or the artist's canvas. Eleonora knew it to be true beyond all knowing. She couldn't prove it but that was of little concern because she was living it. Be Still… and know.

Eleonora carefully got to her feet favoring her left knee. No need. It felt perfect. It took only a glance to confirm that it was perfect. No swelling, no bruising, no pain. In fact, no migraine, no leftover irritation, no fear and no remorse. Eleonora was ready to embrace her new life…but first, that damn file for Whitehead.

As she started toward Y26, the present residence of File No. 47-B from the Late Antiquities Scroll Collection walking was light, effortless as if she were floating across lily pads. She felt well-oiled, frictionless.

However, a few steps further and she noticed the Stillness waning ever so slightly. She seemed to be losing that sense of unity with the objects around her. Each step lost more Stillness. Then she noticed a little tightness in her left knee. She became worried. The specter of Utopia lost darkened her heart, smothered her fire.

Eleonora suddenly noticed her hand was empty, "Where's Whitehead's archival sleeve? Oh! Did I leave it on that box where I sat?" She was sure of it.

Eleonora started back to the box where she had rested her knee and left the archival sleeve. As it came into view Stillness again grew in her awareness. Only lightly at first, then a tickle up her spine. She reached the box, picked up the sleeve.

Her breath caught. Stillness came flooding in. Bubbles of bliss burst in every cell. Her world was love. Not just the love of poets. No. Much more. Ferocious, boundless, palpable. All loves, all things find their home in Stillness. She was home.

Enfolded in the arms of Stillness Eleonora would never again be far from that embrace.

CHAPTER 2

The Manuscript

Eleonora's scientific mind wouldn't rest. Her curiosity a mushroom cloud. How did it happen? Was it the box? Ridiculous! An electromagnetic eruption of some kind? How could she possibly test that? It did seem to pull her to it. Was that just her mind? She wasn't sure. She must know.

She bent over and examined the box closely. It was a squat, dust covered wooden box shoved into a shadowed corner, its edges softened by time. She pushed down on the box testing its durability. The wood creaked, bowed slightly but was sturdy enough. Nothing unusual about that.

She tugged the box out from its corner. The wood rasped across the concrete floor leaving little bits of splintered wood along its path. She ran her fingers along the underside of the lid then lifted. The lid resisted. Would it yield its secret? She tugged with greater will. The box resisted still.

Eleonora stopped, waited just a second. Exasperation exhausted. Stillness returned. The lid yielded with a gentle sigh as air eagerly rushed in. Excited but wary she peered cautiously over the lid and looked inside.

She didn't know what she expected; glowing glyphs, swirling spirits. What she found was unexpected. The expected. Yellowed packing paper crumbling to dust. She ever so cautiously lifted the paper to find a bundle of parchment sheets bound with a frayed grey cord.

Eleonora stiffened, withdrew her hand instinctively. This box, the same box she had sat on, unknowingly — the box where Stillness had found her — was offering her…

Eleonora's hands lay bare her excitement. They trembled slightly as she loosened the cord. The top sheet rolled open as if by the ancient hand that penned it. Aged ink browned to the color of tea. What was that written in humble script? Latin — her eye caught the first line instantly: "Tranquillus esto et scies quod sum."Beneath, a note in Greek. A word in Sanskrit: śūnyatā — emptiness. Nothingness.

Short, quick breaths now, skimming the parchments. Words, unfamiliar and yet known to her, for her. They knew who she was, what she wanted, what she needed. Each word plucked the strings of Stillness. She read,

"To those who discover this — you are not alone in what you feel…"

"Stillness is not created. Stillness is not kept. It is only known."

"Do nothing, and the It will find you."

Her throat tightened, quick contraction, gulped air. Silent, joyful sobbing. Release.

She was not alone. He, this unknown messenger saw her suffering, knew her grief. Had she translated correctly? Was this truly what they said, meant? She considered again.

Eleonora carefully, greedily turned the next pages. Her Latin sufficient, her Greek rusty but usable. The story unfolded:

A monk — unknown but real — had written them. He had known this state. Stillness. Nothingness. His words proved it. Deepened it in her psyche, her heart. Her soul. He described it exactly. Her "box" experience. Small, fretful self, surrendered to boundless untethered Self, beyond hurt. He knew his words would find someone, find her someday, open her to this unexplainable existence beyond words.

Eleonora cradled the parchment as an ancient newborn, pregnant with the wisdom of inner sight. "He knows." She echoed. Through tears of gratitude, "He knows what's happening to me."

The monk continued: "There is no path to Stillness. There is only stopping."

More clarity, more confusion. Doing nothing? Futile laziness?

She sat with those words. Her scientific side, "absurd." She lived science— cataloging, cross-referencing, proving, striving, always striving. Now, crinkled parchment, murmurs from millennia past saying simply, "Do nothing." Absurd! Yet…

She sat hopeful, tentative. The parchment, delicate, definite cradled in her lap. She deliberated. The air stopped moving. Fluorescents stopped trembling. The boxes of files seemed to lean in, listening.

Finally, she decided. She laid the parchment in its crib and covered it with the crumbling yellowed packing paper. She spoke to it as she would the monk, "Wait for me. I'll be back. I will be ready." She closed the lid quietly. Eleonora touched the box warmly as if comforting the wisdom within.

Eleonora sat serenely not really wanting to leave. She thought of Socrates her feline roommate and started to go. She hesitated. Again, she struggled with the idea that nothing had value, much less liberation. What did she know for sure? What she didn't know inspired her and frightened her. Was there danger in this siren Stillness?

She knew the monk existed. He knew what she was feeling. Exactly! He had led her to that experience. Nothing. It kept bouncing around in her head. It just couldn't happen. But it had!

The box. The box had been waiting for her. He had been waiting for her. Waiting almost 2000 years. It wasn't logical. It just didn't make sense. And yet…

Eleonora's thoughts turned thankfully to those of home. There was light and sanctuary and an enigma clothed in fur and claws, welcoming and aloof. This puzzle she warmly welcomed.

CHAPTER 3

The Dream

Eleonora was dreaming. Vivid, alive, physical. She stood atop stone stairs worn unevenly. Decades of monk's shuffling sandals. She felt it first then heard the low, solemn chanting. Vespers ending at the monastery.

Silent brown shadows scattered from the hall their silence betrayed.

Swishing robes, crunching gravel. Heads bowed, occupied, thoughts on salvation or the coming day's chores.

A monk suddenly turned and looked up at Eleonora. The face, deep lines of wisdom and woe. A small teardrop scar at the corner of his eye could not distract from their piercing luminescence.

His face was unknown to her, but she knew what was in his heart.

And then, a sudden shift and her dream became his.

The village was quiet but changing quickly.

He was born beneath limestone cliffs the color of sun-bleached bone, in a village where the river carved a silver ribbon through the dust. His earliest memory was not of his mother's face, but of watching the wind play across the water, dimpling it into patterns he could almost understand. As a boy, he could find the center of stillness in the middle of a marketplace simply by standing and letting the noise pass through him.

The world beyond his village was changing. Merchants from the Kushan Empire spoke of cities where silk flowed like water and spices perfumed the air for days. Along the great roads, languages mingled like currents in a single sea. But in the small stone monastery where he came of age, the outside world was only a rumor carried on the wind. Here, he learned scripture, calligraphy, and the quiet work of tending gardens and mending robes.

His given name, long forgotten by most, meant nothing particular. It was a traveling sage from the East who first called him by a name that stayed: one in his own tongue that meant "space," for the young monk seemed to make room for others simply by being near. Later, when he took full vows in the Christian tradition, he received the name Dometius. He carried both names with ease, like a robe that could be turned inside out.

He had a gift for listening—not the polite, nodding sort, but the kind that made you feel your words were being placed carefully into a bowl for safekeeping. He also had, though he tried to hide it, a small and mischievous wit. Once, when a novice complained about the silence during a week-long fast, Dometius replied, "Then perhaps you should talk less to yourself." The novice, startled, laughed—and so did Dometius.

In the years before his great journey, he heard whispers of a teaching from the East—older than any scripture in their library—about the power of Nothing. Not absence, but a presence so deep it lay beneath thought itself. "Stop. Do nothing," the saying went, "and what you seek will find you." The words lodged in his mind like a seed beneath the soil.

When caravans passed, he listened to travelers speak of far-off lands, of sages who measured time by the breath and claimed the stars could be heard if one grew quiet enough. The world was large, but Dometius knew his path would take him inward before it carried him outward.

The dream began to fade, the cloister dimming to gray. Eleonora felt the cool weight of the stone beneath her feet, the echo of the chant still in her bones. And as she woke, the name she had known in the dream lingered on her lips.

Dometius.

📖 Reflection: A Glimpse of Stillness

- This is not something you need to practice – simply notice the idea. Later, you'll have a chance to experience it for yourself.

- Dometius writes, "In the Nothing, the Stillness will find you." Close your eyes for a single breath. Allow one thought to pass. Notice the small pause before the next thought arrives. However brief, that pause is enough. That is what Dometius discovered.

CHAPTER 4

Nothing

The museum was quieter on Saturdays. No school groups, no curators buzzing in and out of offices, no Grubner hovering to hound her. The hush suited Eleonora. She knew the archives well; they welcomed her.

She had packed almost as if going into the field: a notebook, two pens, a specimen brush, and a small bottle of Dasani reverse osmosis water. Important, she thought, though she usually forgot to open it. A small bag of salt and vinegar chips. Coffee — lots of coffee. Cream, heavy sugar — the essential fuel when the engine was empty. This was no longer mere curiosity. This was research, and Eleonora was ready to take the baton.

She found the box exactly where she had left it, parchments waiting — centuries past — for this moment. The lid lifted without resistance. The parchments lay exactly as before. She took a quiet breath. One hand raised the bundle; the other loosened the gray cord. She spread the sheets on the table beside her pens and notebook. Another breath in, out, and she was ready.

Within the first hour, it appeared — a single word seemed to float above the page. Her breath quickened. In Latin, the monk had written: Methodus.

She bent closer, ready to examine each word in detail, to glean every fragment of wisdom. But instead of diagrams, postures, or invocations, she found only these few instructions:

Sit.

Stop.

Do nothing.

Wait and watch.

What you seek will come from Nothing.

What you seek will find you.

She read them again. Then again. Shook her head as if to clear it.

Was the monk eccentric? Delusional?

"I missed something."

Eleonora translated the lines again, word by word. No mistake — these were the words the monk had penned.

Her neck and shoulders tightened; a migraine began its slow throb behind her eyes. Doing nothing? That wasn't a method. That wasn't work — it was idleness.

"All right," she thought. "If that's what he wants, that's what I'll give him. Nothing."

She pushed her chair back, folded her arms, and stared at the wall.

Minutes passed.

No Nothing.

She glanced around to be sure no one had seen her. Oddly, she felt a little calmer, her thoughts slower, quieter.

"Interesting."

She tried again. "Sit. Stop. Do nothing. Wait and watch." Eyes closed.

After two minutes her nose itched. After five, she wondered if she'd left the stove on. Two minutes later, she was humming tunes from My Fair Lady.

She caught herself. Remembered the monk's instructions and grimaced. "I'm trying. But there's always something going on — thoughts, noises, itchy parts."

A scientist organizes, analyzes, writes peer-reviewed papers. She leaned back. "I'm frazzled. The exact opposite of what the monk promised."

Last night was real. It happened.

Yes — of that she was certain.

Yet she was missing something. She felt it as surely as she had felt the Stillness.

Two thoughts elbowed into her mind: "I'm trying" and "the exact opposite." A shiver. Excitement?

"Have I got it completely backwards?"

The monk had done it. She could, too. She would keep trying. But not tonight.

Home, oolong tea, and an unenthusiastic cat's belly rub awaited.

She bound the parchments gently, returned them to the box, and closed the lid with a soft smile.

"No matter how it turns out," she thought, "I had a phenomenal realization here — a rebirth. I feel it in every pulsing atom of me."

She pushed her chair back, stood, and stretched — and pain like fire shot through her left knee. She yelped, leaned on the table, and fell into the chair.

"Not now," she cried.

Her bag slid to the floor. She slumped, staring ahead… at nothing.

Thoughts came and went: "knee throb… belly rub… monk said…"

Nothing.

She startled — had she slept? No. Her mind was luminously clear. A cloudless sky. Purer than air. Pure Nothing. And within it, Stillness.

She felt full and empty, alive. The flickering lights, the hiss of steam — everything was just right. Stillness.

A thought rose like a bubble:

You did Nothing. You are Stillness.

The monk's words glowed in her mind:

"What you seek will come from Nothing.

What you seek will find you."

She had focused so hard on doing Nothing that she had ignored the last line. You don't walk through the door; you sit, you wait, you watch. And Stillness comes, embraces you, and you are whole.

Love. Light. Laughter.

And Eleonora laughed — deep, rolling, thunderous laughter.

She got it.

CHAPTER 5

Stillness

Her eyes opened slowly, widening with wonder, like a child seeing the sky for the first time. For a moment, the room seemed to shimmer with the same quiet vastness.

Outside the window, a single white feather spiraled upward, turning in the air as though caught in an invisible current. Elenora blinked, uncertain if she had truly seen it or only imagined it. Then it was gone, leaving behind the hush of Stillness within her.

She had found something of inestimable value. A teacher. A companion.

"Hello, my friend," she whispered. Not to the parchment, not to the monk — to Stillness itself.

Eleonora longed to be with Stillness again, to embrace it, and be embraced by it. It was Sunday. The museum was closed, quiet, abandoned — just the way she loved it.

At the side entrance, her key slid easily against the lock's emotionless innards. Click. Snap. The door yielded, and the cool, musty air swept around her.

She stepped quickly inside. One of the museum's great secrets — perhaps the greatest — was waiting. Down the long, narrow corridor, her heels clicked, echoing off damp walls. At the turn by an ancient fire extinguisher, she descended a narrow flight of yellowing concrete stairs. The archive opened its arms.

Her injured knee was a vanishing memory. She threaded quickly to the box, lifted the lid, and set aside the first few pages.

Several new pages came free with surprising ease — unfolding like petals to the sun. One sheet stood apart: the handwriting freer, the paper lighter. At the top, a single Latin word she easily translated: Disciplina.

Instruction.

Her heart quickened. Would this be it — the technique for doing nothing? She took off her glasses, rubbed her eyes, put them back on. Deep breath in, exhale. She leaned closer.

The monk's script read:

"If you would quiet the mind, do not beat it as a stubborn mule, nor bind it like a dog to a post. It will grow sullen and spiritless.

The mind is a monkey. Do not chase the monkey, do not trap it. Offer it a banana and sit. The monkey will come to you, happy to stay."

"What?" She smiled despite herself. "Bananas? Monkeys? Are you kidding me?" She shook her head, glanced up at the ceiling, then back at the page.

She kept reading.

"The banana is simple noticing. See what is there — a sound, a thought, an itch. Do not hold it. Do not push it away. Only watch. The mind enjoys being watched — it will bring you more.

Between the comings and goings, there will be gaps — moments when nothing appears. Do not leap at them. Do not think, 'I have found it!' Watch. Wait. Only this.

Within the Nothing, Stillness is waiting. When you wait in the Nothing, the Stillness will come to you. This Stillness was not empty silence — it was the living fullness that could later blossom into peace, joy, even love. Seeds waiting to flower. The Stillness will reveal itself."

Eleonora held the parchment to the light, as if some hidden wisdom might appear. She read the lines again… and again.

A picture formed in her mind: she was sitting at the monk's feet, full of enthusiasm, peppering him with questions before he could answer — wanting to grab a monkey by the tail and make him sit. Just as she had done yesterday.

The monk, smiling through kind eyes, plucked a banana from above his head and handed it to her.

Smiling inwardly, she laid the parchment aside, leaned back in the chair, and — as instructed — let her mind wander wherever it wanted.

She noticed first how tightly she was closing her eyes. The squeak of the exhaust fan came, then faded. A faint whiff of coffee passed. She felt a flicker of agitation and watched it dissolve… and then she was gone.

Nothing.

Her breathing so faint it barely existed. How long had she been there? No way to know. No time. No space. Nothing.

Then — the Stillness.

She remembered the monk's words:

"Within the Nothing, Stillness is waiting. When you wait in the Nothing, the Stillness will come to you. This Stillness was not empty silence — it was the living fullness that could later blossom into peace, joy, even love. Seeds waiting to flower."

Not with Nothing — within the Nothing. Not the absence of movement or sound, but something deeper. Profound. All-permeating.

And for the first time, she understood: the banana is simple noticing, awareness. Stillness is its essence.

She giggled at the strangeness, at how natural it felt.

Opening her eyes, she let a small, incredulous laugh escape.

"Bananas," she said again — softer now, with Stillness in her words.

CHAPTER 6

Practice

Eleonora didn't wait for another weekend. She couldn't.

By Monday night, she was sitting cross-legged on her narrow couch, a copy of the monk's instructions propped against a pillow.

Eleonora avoided technology like the plague. The one invasion she allowed was her iPhone Pro Max, which she used to make copies of what she now thought of as her manuscripts.

Socrates was draped across her lap like a soggy burrito. Her fingers massaged his fur absently as she read aloud:

"See what is there. A sound, a thought, an itch."

"An itch?" she murmured, scratching the back of her neck.

Socrates grumbled, got up, turned around, huffed once, and reclaimed his spot on her lap.

Eleonora began again. "A sound, a thought…"

Expecting Nothing, she closed her eyes. She waited for sounds, for itches, for whatever else might step into line. She watched. She waited. For only a moment, Nothing tapped her on the shoulder — barely noticed, but there. A growing sense of well-being spread through her.

The phone rang. "Who would be calling at this time of night?" She glanced at her watch. 9:53 PM. The call went to voicemail.

She closed her eyes again. Watching. Waiting. Thoughts came unbidden. She stayed the disinterested observer. Watching…

She startled — eyes open, breath catching. Everything looked the same, yet brighter, livelier, friendlier. Socrates looked up at her, much as the monk had done in her dream. He knew.

She thought, I should find out who called. She checked her watch. 10:47 PM. Fifty-four minutes! I was… what? Not asleep. Not unconscious. Awake — aware of Nothing. Aware of the screen before the movie begins.

She never found out who called.

Tuesday morning, Eleonora was back in the archives. She'd snuck away between meetings, eager to practice Nothing. She found the box that held the parchments. She sat, feeling the wood bow gently beneath her — welcoming her.

A slow inhale, an easy exhale. Eyes closed. It came quickly now: muffled echoes from the hall, two colleagues whispering about some exciting new discovery, footsteps fading away… Nothing.

She saw it more clearly now. It wasn't the absence of something. It was the fullness of Nothing — the richness between breaths, the unfathomable depth between heartbeats. The winter that births a bountiful spring.

Her eyes opened softly. The archives hadn't changed — except to her. Something inside her stirred, germinating quietly. A small, steady joy hummed in her chest. So still. So delicate. So unbroken she almost missed it.

Eleonora was reviving.

Wednesday morning. Kitchen table. A cup of steaming Oolong. Another session brewing. Socrates sprawled lazily across the manuscript page.

"Are you guarding our secrets, Socrates? Are the secrets of Stillness safe under your sleepy gaze?"

He looked at her through half-closed eyes, as if to say, Who else?, and rested his head between his paws.

Eleonora sat beside him, her hand resting gently on his back. She closed her eyes and followed his lead — the disinterested observer. Watching. Waiting.

It took almost no time at all now. The well-traveled road: the aroma of Oolong, the ticking stove, the sun warming her bare arm. She took no interest in them. She knew what was coming and welcomed it. It did not disappoint.

It was not falling. It was not expanding. It was... nothing. Beyond description. Beyond thought. Beyond belief. Only that it felt good. At home. Like an old friend — never demanding, only serving.

Socrates sighed, curling around her hand in a feline hug. She felt him. He knew Nothing. They shared it — a bond between species.

"Hey, big fella," she said, tousling his fur. "You knew all along, didn't you?"

Socrates didn't answer. He simply stopped licking his paw and regarded her casually. She thought, so that's what a smug cat looks like.

By Friday, Eleonora no longer needed to sit and close her eyes. Nothing was everywhere — walking, driving, eating, brushing her teeth. She found special joy with Socrates; they shared Nothing and became stronger together.

She felt lighter, more energetic, friendlier — as if the hurt others offered could not touch her. This, she would soon discover, was exactly what she needed to navigate the troubled waters ahead.

📖 Practice: Waiting for the Next Thought

- Sit comfortably, eyes closed. Watch your thoughts as they come and go. Now ask yourself: Where will my next thought come from?

- Wait. Notice the space that opens as you wait. That space is Nothing.

- You can play with this question in many ways: What color will my next thought be? What shape? What will it feel like? Smell like?

- Each time you wait, there is a moment of stillness before the thought arrives. Rest there. That brief pause is the beginning of Nothing.

CHAPTER 7

Something More

Dometius needed time to himself, away from the monastery.

Deep in thought, he began to climb the hill. Thinking. Climbing. Thinking. He stopped and looked back, surprised to see the monastery a pebble by the side of the road.

Up here the breeze was cooler. The grass greener. His thoughts clearer. The goats grazed contentedly, their bells unwilling to defile the stillness.

He lay back in the thick grass, his head cradled in the roots of an ancient Aleppo pine. Burnt-orange cones swayed in the breeze, needles scratching at a pale blue sky. A wary crow watched him with one eye.

He was free. No predawn chanting. No stables to clean. No hungry monks clamoring at meals. The goats needed nothing. He needed Nothing.

Dometius liked monastic life. It simply didn't deliver what it promised. He was learning that you cannot work your way into heaven. He'd seen it in the ascetics of India — enduring great hardship only made for a grumpy guru.

He was learning to do Nothing. But what was Nothing?

That word — Nothing. What did it mean? Formless. Motionless. No handle for the mind. It did not exist, yet it gave life to life.

The masters of the East never tried to define it. "Futile," they said. "A fool's game." Instead, they pointed another way: Don't define. Don't understand. Be an enduring flower, and the bee will come to you. Watch. Wait.

A wisp of wind swayed the branches, sunlight splashing across his thoughts. What if…

Wonder. Expectation. Dometius sat upright against the tree trunk and closed his eyes gently. The outer world dissolved. His attention turned inward.

He began watching his thoughts with easy attention — a cat at a mouse hole. Waiting. Watching. There! Between the thoughts — a brief moment of… Nothing.

…thoughts… thoughts… thoughts… again, Nothing. The briefest of moments.

A knowing smile spread, forcing his eyes open. Attention is the banana. Thoughts the monkey. Nothing the sublime taste of the banana. Hunger satisfied.

He had it. The technique. It wasn't about pushing out sound or sensation. Liberation was in yielding. He couldn't stop smiling — not just for the joy of Nothing, but for the absurd simplicity of it. This innocent realization could satisfy the hunger of humanity.

He whispered to himself, "Now the monks will have something to sing about."

In the East, the masters spoke in mindless riddles. They preached effortlessness, but their practice was arduous.

"It takes years of practice to clear the mind of thought," they would say — then twist the body, force the breath, and beat the mind into submission. Yes, it took years.

But here, under the Aleppo pine, Dometius knew better.

Inspired, he rose suddenly. The crow screeched and took flight, leaving a single black feather at his feet.

From a leather pouch, he drew his writings. Walking to a flat rock, he knelt and began to write in his fine script:

If you would find the Nothing, do not command it to appear. Let your mind wander where it will. Watch gently, as you would watch a child at play. See each thought come, see it go. Between the coming and the going, there is a space. Wait there. In that space, Nothing rests. In the Nothing, the Stillness will find you. And from that Stillness, I feel that greater qualities may yet bloom, though their names are hidden from me.

He lifted his pen and read the words. They were true. The process revealed. Simple. Unassuming. Perfect. Belief was unnecessary. Years of practice — an absurdity. Instant. Effortless.

Future travelers of the spirit might brush it aside. Mystical fantasies, they would say. There can be no salvation without suffering!

Let them.

He knew what they did not: Nothing worked — and now he could reveal it.

📖 Practice: Finding Nothing

- Step 1: Let your mind wander where it will.

- Step 2: Watch gently.

- Step 3: See each thought come and go.

- Step 4: Between them, notice the space.

- Step 5: Rest there. In that space, Nothing rests.

Deeper Background: When Nothing Works Try Doing Nothing by Frank Kinslow

CHAPTER 8

Eufeeling

The archives were almost empty the next morning. Slanted windows, clear sunlight greying as it strained through archival dust. The aging light laid placidly across floorboards and long tables. Resting. The steam pipe remembered Eleonora and hissed hello. A misplaced bird flew to the light above.

Eleonora back at the box wondering what drew her here so early this morning. She had no plan. Just a quiet voice encouraging her to visit her old friend. Somehow with the parchments came quiet comfort.

With reverence she lifted them from their nest and laid them on the table. As she leafed through the last few pages, near the bottom a mainly ragged leaf, curled and cracked caught her eye. She brought it to the light and bent closer.

Not much to this short passage. Yet the words somehow moved her. Lit her up. Excitement. A sense of completion. The click of a hasp driven home.

"In the Nothing, the Stillness will find you. And from that Stillness, greater qualities may yet bloom."

Greater Qualities!

What qualities?

A memory rose: the couch; Socrates warm and heavy; the phone ringing, unanswered; the way the room had grown brighter, friendlier, for no reason she could name. Another memory: the kitchen, Oolong steam ribboning past her cheek, sunlight on her forearm; the soft, good quiet that had slipped between her thoughts and then— without drama—spread outward.

Was that it? Not sure.

Like a fresh dream the memory was vibrant in her mind. She lived it without understanding. Didn't have to. Stillness had moved in to stay. As real as the parchment in her hands.

These words named it. Left it free to fly. Between the coming and the going, there is a space. The space where Nothing dwelled.

She'd gotten it. Something ancient deep within her clicked. Eleonora had been holding her breath. She exhaled.

She surveyed the archives. A maintenance worker just leaving with his folded ladder under one arm. A colleague, at the furthest corner captivated by the contents of his box. Perfect!

She could try it now. No preparation needed. Nothing was a frequent friend. All she had do is follow the monk's instructions.

She anchored the corner of the parchment with her phone. Sat comfortably. Looked around the archive. Eleonora left her eyes open this time. Inner thoughts or outer thoughts, all the same. A breath in. A breath out.

Let your mind wander where it will.

At first it was visually noisy. To her left, a map of ancient Constantinople, frame slanted. Bird still fluttering, freedom denied. Colleague motionless, captivated.

Then, inner quietness, outer order. All things seem to be bound by a silent steadiness. What she saw became a thought. Thoughts began to flow. She mentally retreated. The quiet observer.

See each thought come, see it go.

They came—neat, muddled, routine—and went. She waited, the way you wait for a cherished friend soon to arrive. And then, an emptiness of thought. A fullness of… not emptiness.

Almost unseen: a small, perfectly unremarkable pause in which the whole room seemed to rest. Not absence. A fullness without burden. Freedom.

Wait there.

Waiting. Natural. The uninvolved witness. A gentle, pervading ease.

Nothing. Stillness. Something more.

The word, a wave on the ocean of awareness swelled then settled again. Nothing. She didn't stay with Nothing The easy watcher. Stillness awoke. Stayed with her. Something more.

The eyes of the easy watcher fell on the parchment in front of her. And Nothing. Stillness. Something more. From the campus tower the bell chimed the hour and Nothing. Stillness. Something more. Her colleague collected his papers, heels clacking down the narrow hall. Nothing. Stillness. Something more. The bird was still.

Then a tender change came soft as mist. Loving as a mother's embrace. Compassion had come to stay. Asking nothing. Bestowing Nothing and... What was this something?

How could it be; Nothing and something? Nothing and peace, and joy, and compassion, grace, bliss, gratitude, and love. Nothing and love?

Confused Eleonora needed to know, "What is this fullness beyond Nothing? What name?" No answer.

She thought of Socrates and what they shared just the other night. Warm belly, soft fur, and that smug look that simultaneously protested and encouraged. They had become closer since they shared Nothing and this...

something. He would like what she has learned. She wondered if he already knew.

She read the lines again.

In the Nothing, the Stillness will find you.

The phrase rang like singing crystal. Pure. Stirring.

"Eufeeling," she whispered with some surprise. It was not on the parchment. It came from her. From somewhere ancient, newly granted. It was hers.

Eufeeling.

No words could hold Eufeeling. Then she thought, "Will it stay? Will Eufeeling come with me?"

She stood uncertainly as if holding a priceless artifact. Careful not to break the spell. Eufeeling remained. She inhaled slowly. Bubbles of bliss burst inside her. Overwhelming.

Eleonora walked to the far window. Eufeeling went with her. Each step reverberated unbearable joy. Her silk blouse sliding over her upper arms, the shushing steam pipe, the gentle sloshing of the custodians mop all sources of remarkable joy. She heard the bird's slapping wings and looked up. In that moment it slipped through the broken glass and was free.

She returned to the table and sat. The parchment did not glow or speak to her. It was simply what it was. A stone for stepping into Eufeeling.

She understood, not in words, that this was what could move into the world. Not with violence of effort. Trying unnecessary. Eufeeling was enough.

The light from the windows was softening. The bird returned to his nest. Somewhere a door shut softly, and the building fell silent. Waiting.

Eleonora smoothed the parchment with the back of her fingers. As gentle smile. She silently acknowledged the brilliance that was Dometius. And the anonymous hands that had stored and numbered and preserved this leaf. For the ridiculous luck of being alive today.

She copied the lines into her notebook in her own hand. They were fine and full and true. They did not glow or speak. They were what they where.

If you would find the Nothing, do not command it to appear.

Let your mind wander where it will.

Watch gently.

See each thought come, see it go.

Between the coming and the going, there is a space.

Wait there.

In that space, Nothing rests.

In the Nothing, the Stillness will find you.

When she finished, she added Nothing and something more:

Eufeeling.

The ordinary world assembled itself around her with its usual competence: dust, wood, letters, light. Inside that ordinary, a new usefulness had arrived, like a tool you did not know you owned until someone placed it in your hand and said, Try this.

She capped her pen and for a moment sat very still. Then she lay the parchment in its bed. It had done its work for today. Eleonora was not practicing now, not doing. Standing, she felt Eufeeling watching, waiting. She consented. Eufeeling had come to stay.

She stepped through the door and paused. Waiting for Eufeeling to catch up. Always a step ahead, Eufeeling was waiting in the hall.

Down the corridor, tired voices, shuffling feet, cold coffee. This was Eleonora's challenge. Only, she did not know it yet.

There would be people to face. There would be stormy seas. The world would continue unchanged. For awhile.

She smiled and went to meet it.

The Gate

Morning air, cool and sharp. The kind that stops the first breath halfway.

Eleonora stepped out of her building, pulled up her coat collar and hunched against the wind.

Eufeeling warmed her. Not metaphor.

A presence. There when she remembered. There when she didn't.

Light as a scarf. Warm as sunlight.

She didn't rush.

Her shoes clicked dully on the wet sidewalk.

A bus roared past, grey-black exhaust scattering leaves at her feet.

She watched them tumble and swirl like happy children.

In the distance an elevated train clacked and hissed.

The city moved around her.

Eufeeling moved with.

A man, late for his coffee, stepped in front of Eleonora.

She stopped abruptly. Looking up.

He mumbled and went into the café ahead of her.

Eleonora smiled and surprised herself.

She entered the café on the corner.

Warm blast of air, jumbled bodies, jumbled voices.

The barista, looking over bobbing heads called out,

"Same as always?"

Eleonora smiled.

"Yes, thank you."

Her voice warmer than she expected. Surprised. Again

The barista's answering smile also a surprise.

Waiting for her coffee, she noticed a fly on the windowsill.

Sluggish, he seemed lost. Wrong season. Near his end.

She bent closer. Too frail to fly. She felt him watching.

She felt a kind of cosmic sadness.

Cherishing hot coffee at her desk, Eleonora normally hurried back to the museum.

Despite the cold, she strolled.

Winter weary sunlight half-heartedly lit her way.

Coffee in hand, she walked the block to the museum.

Even in the weak sun the marbled museum steps shone proudly.

"Come Ye All and Wonder."

A passing cloud.

The steps, tired and old waited patiently. This too shall pass.

She hurried up the stairs. Lively strides. Not her usual self.

Just at the top the sun returned. The tall glass doors ignited.

She stopped. A strange thought, "The doors. They are my gate."

She smiled at the image of the walls inside glowing gold. Floors humming hymnals.

She entered.

The acrid smell of burnt coffee was first. Then scuffling feet on scratched tiled floors. Now was the soft, lively murmuring. By day's end a monotonous drone.

No glowing walls. No hummed hymnals. Business as usual.

Except for Eufeeling.

She turned the corner to her office and walked right into Ben.

Coffee sloshing, not spilling. Her hand slapping against his chest.

His face registered surprise. Then caution. Then it relaxed.

He saw it. The change. She was softer yet sturdier. Bolder. Kinder. Transcendent.

"You're early," he said. A little too harsh.

"I wanted to get started," she replied. A little too quick.

Silence.

He started to speak, jaw muscles tensing slightly. Nothing.

She hesitated, turned and continued down the hall to her office.

Ben wanted to know what happened to Eleonora. Same face. Same body.

No anger. No frustration. Confident.

Something wonderful was working inside her.

He had to know.

She rewound their meeting. His face. Surprised, yes. But wonder? Admiration?

She was also surprised. His body. Firmer.

"Funny," she thought. "What happened to Eufeeling back there?"

Eleonora approached the archives with anticipation. Her place of rebirth. Her womb.

She embraced the everywhere dust, the dank, musty air. Even the flickering fluorescents.

The monk's parchments waited for her. In their folder. In the box.

CHAPTER 10

Eufeeling Escapes

The next morning, Eleonora arrived earlier than usual. She loved the permeating sense of solitude. The stillness. Familiar. Comfortable like old shoes. It was her museum. Her friend. She swept lightly down its halls, past darkened offices to her own.

Eufeeling moved with her. In essence, was her.

She breezed into her office flipped on the light put her purse and notebook on the desk then sat down to a promising day...

"My coffee!"

Ben caught up to her in the Eureka Café down the street, where the air was thick with the smell of espresso and the tink-rattle of spoon in empty cup.

"Eleonora!"

Surprised at her name, she turned quickly and pressed into Ben for a second time.

Embarrassed.

Eufeeling forgotten? Waiting? Watching?

Early enough they found a quiet table in the corner. Hesitant exchange. Both careful. Watchful.

Several times, Eleonora saw Ben rubbing his shoulder. She looked at it, then quizzically at him.

Been smiled sheepishly, "An old rowing injury."

Without thinking, Eleonora reached across the table and lightly laid her hand on his forearm. Eufeeling was there. Eleonora was Eufeeling.

Ben stopped mid-sentence. Still. Waiting. The wrinkles in his forehead smoothing. Shoulders sloping.

"What…what was that?" He whispered, leaning forward.

"Nothing," she said. "Just Nothing."

They both knew it was more.

Later that day, on her way back from the archives, Eleonora ran into Carla from Collections. Carla was rubbing the side of her neck, wincing. "Too much time over the restoration table," she said with a weary smile.

Eleonora laid her hand on Carla's shoulder. Almost immediately the pain and tension emptied from Carla's face. Then surprise. Then a smile. "That was... I mean, wow! It's all better."

"Enjoy." Eleonora smiled and walked away.

On her way out of the museum Eleonora stopped by the security office to return the key to the storage room. Frank, a guard who had been with the museum longer than some of the objects stored in the archives, sat one leg resting on a file crate.

"Fell off my motorcycle." He offered sheepishly. "Rain makes it worse."

Eleonora rolled over a second chair. She placed her hand lightly above the knee, looked kindly into his eyes. A sudden breath then his breathing became still. Several long heartbeats. Frank got to his feet and cautiously challenged the knee.

"Hey." He said, "It doesn't hurt." He turned to the guard watching the monitors, "Hey Bill, look." When he turned back around Eleonora was gone.

Eleonora stayed late at the museum. On her way home she stopped at the café for a quick cup. The evening sounds were more subdued but still semi-chaotic; baristas calling out orders, blistering espresso machines, clinking cups on saucers around weary sunset gossip. The smudged beige speakers on the walls offered classical music that no one heard.

Ben was there too, leaning over a book.

Eleonora ordered a cup of oolong tea and a butterscotch cookie. She sat looking out the window at nothing. Her tea and cookie ignored. The little café found Eufeeling. The noise lost its edge, softened. The room gave a collective sigh. Conversations eased. Even the espresso machine seemed to whisper. The speakers were playing Beethoven's Lullaby.

Ben, feeling the change, looked up from his book. Their eyes met. Recognition. Nothing was said. Something unmoving within them, moved.

Eleonora left the café. Eufeeling hugging her then spreading its wings, touching all that she could see, all that she could know. And could not know. The sun just set. Ribbons of red and purple laced the sky. Beautiful. But what of tomorrow?

CHAPTER 11

The Technique

The archives were still as stone. Watching. Waiting.

Ben tripped along behind Eleonora. Too close. To anxious.

Nervously, "Why are we here?"

Eleonora kept walking. Not talking. Eyes on the box.

"I don't know what you've been doing," he said nervously, "but it's working." "People are talking," he muttered. Needing the distraction.

At a familiar table, now set with two chairs, the box with the monk's parchments waited. Pages already spread.

She laid her hand on the box. Beside it, a white feather lifted gently into the air — though no draft stirred.

"You know, the change you've noticed. The healing." She helped.

"Healing?" Ben tilted his head further. "From what?"

"From everything." She pulled out a chair. "Sit."

He hesitated. "What are you going to do? You're going to tell me, or show me?"

Her lips curved. "Show you."

Ben sat.

"Now close your eyes and let your mind wander wherever it wants to go." She instructed.

Ben's eyes closed. The lids fluttered as if they hadn't decided. Finally, the movement stopped, his lids relaxed.

"Now become aware of your thinking. The content is not important. Just watch your thoughts, how easily they come and go."

Ben's face tensed slightly, as if concentrating.

"No need to try. Watch your thoughts as you'd watch a movie. Watch your thoughts flow easily across the screen of your mind."

The strain in his face eased. A soft sigh.

"Thinking is like speaking. It has pauses, little breaks where there is Nothing. Watch for those pauses."

Eleonora waited. Ben's shoulders sloped. His breath steadied.

"The pause may be brief. A second or two. That's enough. Watch and wait for the Nothing."

"When thoughts return, simply watch again. Wait for the next pause. The Nothing between them."

She paused, giving him time.

"Remember, Ben — you are a disinterested observer. No trying. No effort. Just watch and wait."

After a while she added, "Don't push thoughts away. Don't cling to Nothing. Innocent observation. No expectations."

Ben's body slackened. Breath quiet. His face like a child's in sleep.

"Excellent," she said softly. "Wait and watch, Ben. Nothing more. Wait and watch."

She let him continue another minute. Then:

"We're finished. Come back slowly. The first times with Nothing can be disorienting."

Ben opened his eyes as though waking from a dream he didn't want to leave. "Eleonora... this is remarkable. You are remarkable.

A pause. She took a breath. "Call me Ellie."

Something shifted in his expression — not surprise, recognition.

"Ellie," he said softly. "Thank you."

His eyes moved to the parchments, then back to her. "What do you call that?"

Her lips curved around it. "Eufeeling. I call it the Eufeeling Technique."

She said it simply, but the weight of it reached back to the monk who had only hinted at 'something more.' What was promised then, she was now naming.

He nodded slowly, tucking the name away.

He was beginning to understand the weight of what she had found — and the strength it would take to hold it.

She breathed deeply, ready for a new day.

📖 Practice: The Eufeeling Technique

What Ellie showed Ben is not hidden away in archives — it can be discovered directly, here and now. Eufeeling reveals itself when we stop trying to reach for it.

Sit comfortably

No special posture. Simply be at ease.

Watch your thoughts

Thoughts may drift where they will. This wandering is not a problem — it is the way in.

Wait for the gap

Between thoughts or sensations, tiny pauses appear. Moments of nothing. From it, a softness or fullness may show itself. That is Eufeeling.

Rest there lightly

Don't grasp or hold it. Just notice, and rest when it appears.

Return naturally

When thoughts return, easily watch and wait for the Nothing between them. Eufeeling will surface in its own time.

Ellie's reminder: "You don't force Eufeeling. You notice it — and it carries you."

Deeper background: *Awefeeling; How You Can Decrease Pain, Break Negative Patterns, and Find Peace in Only 31/2 Minutes a Day* by Frank Kinslow

Also: *The Eufeeling Technique* by Frank Kinslow

Audio Download (KinslowSystem.com)

CHAPTER 12

Ripples

A ruby-red cardinal woke Ben with pure tones of gladness. Its mate, drab brown, sang in harmony. For the first time in months, he felt deeply rested.

Warm sunlight pressed against his eyelids. *Wake up,* it seemed to say. *The best is yet to come.*

He stretched, yawned, opened his eyes. The day waited.

Sun Salutation. Backstretch, arms extended. No shoulder pain. *Whose body did I wake up in?* He touched his palms to the floor. Shaved a face fifteen years younger than yesterday's. Couldn't stop smiling, even with toothpaste dribbling.

Today he broke routine. Instead of rushing, he sat in his overstuffed chair — arms hugging him like family. The perfect companion for this day.

His first solo Eufeeling Technique.

He sat. Exhaled. Closed his eyes.

Watched. Waited. Disinterested observer.

It began immediately. Expansion. Lightness.

Bubbles of bliss. Balanced. Complete. No hunger. No hurry.

Only: *I Am.*

Always before, a mad dash to the café. Today he sauntered. Amused at chaos and clatter. Amused at his own quiet. Coffee in hand, he strolled toward the museum. Toward Ellie.

Ellie moved down the row of offices.

"Good morning, Tiffany."

Tiffany, just back from her honeymoon, sat with wadded tissues. Red-rimmed eyes, nose running.

"Good morning, Eleonora," she sniffled.

Ellie drew up a chair. "Why the tears, Tiff?"

"Justin doesn't love me. He wants to go out with his friends on our three-week anniversary."

"Give me your hand." Ellie wrapped Tiffany's hands in hers.

"Shhh. Let your mind wander."

Ellie yielded to Eufeeling. Tiffany yielded too.

The office hushed. Outside noises dimmed. Tiffany's sobs slowed. Breath deepened.

Then it was over. Eyes clear, full of wonder.

"What did you… how? Eleonora, I feel — free. I'm not afraid."

"That's Eufeeling, Tiffany. It makes everything better. Now I've got to get to work."

She spoke it lightly, but these were the same depths Dometius had only glimpsed across centuries: the Something More that blooms from Stillness.

Across the centuries, another ripple formed.

Dometius swept courtyard stones. Eufeeling pooled there, subtle eddies crowding the square. All who entered felt it.

A cry beyond the walls. A boy clutching his goat — its leg bent at an unnatural angle. The family's only income, broken. The boy wept. The goat bleated.

Dometius knelt. Took the boy's hand, placed both hands on the leg. The boy quieted. The goat stilled.

"Splint the leg, Dometius," one monk barked. "Quit fooling around."

"Give it a chance," Dometius muttered.

Before their eyes the leg straightened. Whole again.

Dometius lifted the goat, handed it back.

"Now splint it. It will heal straight."

The boy tugged at his robe, eyes shining, smile like sun. Then he ran, disturbing the dust.

Dometius returned to his broom. Younger monks pressed close with questions. Older ones whispered. *Trouble. Lines are being drawn.*

Back in Chicago, Ben leaned into Ellie's office. Luminous face, radiant smile. She smiled back before she could stop herself. Yesterday they had shared Eufeeling. Today they shared something more.

Ellie felt it. Liked it. Grew cautious. *Not now. Not if it pulls me away from Eufeeling.*

Ben felt it too, with no restraint.

"Ellie, meet me after work. Let's talk."

"I'm not sure, Ben. I…"

"Come on. About Eufeeling. Meet me at the café."

She hesitated, then nodded. "I have some ideas."

The café corner. Small round table. Two wire chairs. Two expectant souls.

Ellie arrived late. Ben waved. She quickened her pace, faster than she meant to. "Hi." Purse on chair, notebook on table. She looked into Ben's eyes —

A jolt. Soft electricity. Flowing tenderness. She looked away quickly, down at her notebook. Broke the spell.

The café's clatter faded. Only the two of them remained.

Ben's voice trembled with wonder.

"Today has been a wonderful day. Like no other. Eufeeling is — no words. It's in me, around me. It is me. I… Ellie, help me out here."

She smiled, knowing.

"Ellie, you've discovered something profound. Can you imagine how many people could be helped? Can you teach more than one at a time? What kinds of suffering can it cure? Children? Animals? Could it work at a distance? Is it spiritual? Could it —"

"Hold it, hold it, Ben." Ellie laughed. "Your brain must be boiling."

"The short answer is, I don't know. I've been paying attention mostly to Nothing, and to something even deeper… Stillness."

"Stillness?"

"Another time," she waved. "As for what Eufeeling can do. I don't know. I'm as new to this as you are."

Ben leaned closer. "Ellie… do you want to find out?"

"Yes," she said, surprised at her own warmth. "I do."

--------   --------   --------   --------   --------

📖 Reflection: Stillness and Eufeeling

Nothing is the gate. Stillness is the inner kingdom. And Eufeeling is living in that kingdom — the kingdom alive within you. They are not three separate things but one unfolding: the way in, the heart of it, and the life that breaths it.

CHAPTER 13

True Feeling

The reading room at the Eureka Café. Small circle. Curious faces.

Ellie stood at the front, steady but nervous. Ben sat in the back, quiet.

She breathed.

"You've all touched Eufeeling. Tonight, I want to share more. Questions first?"

Tiffany's hand shot up.

"Why do you call it Eufeeling?"

"I wanted a name that carried truth. Eu — from the Greek — means true, genuine, real. We enter Stillness through the gate of Nothing. We express Stillness through Eufeeling.

Eufeeling is the pure reflection of Stillness, like white light passing through a prism and unfolding into colors. You are that prism. The pure light of Stillness becomes the colors of Eufeeling, love, bliss, gratitude as it shines through you. Eufeeling may appear as many, yet it is always one — a single true reflection of Stillness."

Nods. Pens scribbled.

The HR woman raised her hand.

"What do you mean, true feeling? How can it not be an emotion?"

"That's a good question. Eufeeling isn't an emotion at all. It's the source of emotion. When you rest in it, pure feelings come — peace, joy, compassion, love. Not forced. Just radiating. Like sunlight after clouds."

The room hushed. Even the barista leaned in.

"Close your eyes. Let thoughts wander. Watch them drift. Don't force. Don't chase. When a pause comes, wait there. That is the doorway."

Chairs creaked. Breaths slowed. One smiled softly. Another's lip quivered. Tiffany sighed. Frank sat upright, listening.

Minutes passed.

"Now open your eyes."

They blinked back into the room, each carrying something different. Tiffany looked lighter. The HR woman whispered, "Strange, but calm." The barista shrugged. "I don't know if anything happened."

Frank rubbed his hands, said nothing. His face was still.

The group disbanded. Ben lingered behind.

"Ellie… when I try it, nothing happens. I'm not sure I'm doing it right."

She touched his arm.

"Don't try. Just watch. Wait. Let it come when it will. Eufeeling doesn't need effort—it just needs space."

He nodded slowly, still unsure but steadier.

Ellie gathered her notes. The room glowed faintly. For the first time she felt it: she wasn't just learning. She was teaching.

CHAPTER 14

Stillness Waiting

The monastery courtyard was dusty, hushed. Heat shimmered on pale stone. A shabby broom leaned forgotten against the wall.

A handful of younger monks clustered around Dometius — eager, guarded, unsure.

"Do not grasp," he told them, eyes twinkling. "Mist settles on the open palm. Watch. Thoughts stop. Wait…"

One monk startled upright, guilty at drifting to sleep. Another frowned. "Nothing. I feel nothing."

Dometius smiled gently. "Good. That is a beginning."

Later that day, two novices carried the teaching beyond the cloister.

At the roadside, a farmer knelt by a broken wheel, face twisted with pain. Unable to stand. One novice touched his shoulder.

The farmer rose. Wonder bloomed where pain had been. Gratefulness shone.

In a nearby village, a fevered child moaned in her sleep. The second novice placed his palm on her chest. Breathing eased. The fever broke. Peaceful sleep.

The villagers whispered. The whispers returned to the monastery.

The elders frowned. "Recklessness. This will bring disgrace."

But still—the whispers spread.

Ellie stood in the reading room at the Eureka Café. A smaller circle: Tiffany, Frank, Barb the barista, Helen from HR.

They settled in, expectant. Ben sat apart, watchful.

Ellie, more confident now, cleared her throat. "Before we go further, let's begin with a few minutes of the Eufeeling Technique you learned last week."

They nodded. Tiffany's smile was radiant.

They began. Peace settled quickly, soft and tangible, spilling into the room.

After a few minutes Ellie spoke, voice barely above a breath. "That… that felt good." She surprised herself with the warmth in her tone. "Didn't it?"

Nods answered her. Quiet smiles glowed. Something like fellowship blossomed.

"You've all held Eufeeling," she continued. "Now I'd like you to give it away. However you feel to. Whenever you like. If you see someone hurting, share it with them as I did with you. Next week, tell me what you found."

Frank looked hesitant. Tiffany eager. Barb tapped her pen, already imagining. Helen pensive.

They left together, buoyed by the sense of sharing an open secret.

Ben rocked back in his chair, brimming with enthusiasm.

Ellie caught his look. "Easy, Ben. Wait and watch."

He exhaled, grinning sheepishly.

"Yes, teacher."

Later, the sun's last rays splashed the windows fire-red. Ben and Ellie strolled slowly, shadows overlapping.

"You were born to teach," he said warmly.

Ellie bristled. Praise never sat easily. She wanted to dismiss it. But his steady certainty made something glow inside. She turned away, so he wouldn't see.

"Eleonora!"

The word cracked through the hallway like a whip. Ellie froze.

Dr. Grubner loomed, arms folded, disgust carved deep.

"Don't waste the museum's time playing guru," he spat. Finger wagging. "Return to your cataloguing."

Her shoulders slumped. The timid shadow returned.

But Ben stood beside her, steady. Silent.

Grubner shot him a warning look and stalked away.

That night, Ellie sat alone, thoughts tumbling. Grubner's vehemence. Her job at stake? Could she give up Eufeeling? Could she let Ben be drawn into his crosshairs?

Ben rose in her mind. Soft sunshine. His care. His compassion. His steadying presence. She could not let harm come to him.

Her heart raced. What to do? What to…

She closed her eyes.

Her thoughts stumbled, slowed, dissolved. Even her breath seemed to forget itself.

Then— Something. Wider than joy. Deeper than peace. A vastness that held her, infinite, inviolate. Sacred.

It touched her. At first a whisper.

Soon, a tempest.

Eufeeling.

In the cafeteria, a tray slipped; forks clattered. A young intern flushed, embarrassed.

Ben's hand found her shoulder. "It's okay. Breathe."

She steadied, calmer than she expected.

"Thank you." Her eyes lingered, curious.

Ben stood awkward, unsettled. He hadn't meant to give anything. It just happened.

Later, at his desk, Ben replayed the morning. Was he supposed to feel this good? So good that others noticed? Eufeeling was working in ways he had never dreamed.

He thought of past bursts of happiness: first love, second love, childhood birthdays. But those moments always had a cause — and causes change. Loves fade. Joy melts like ice on hot pavement.

"Why doesn't happiness last?" he wondered. "Conditional exuberance." He chuckled.

Then it struck him. Those highs had always carried a frantic edge, leaving exhaustion in their wake. They were full — but left him empty.

Empty, but not Nothing.

He gazed out the window, reflective.

Suddenly he was four again. A bent twig dragged through dirt. Lines in the soil, runny nose, dirt in his shoes.

Eufeeling.

Bathtub play.

Candy on his tongue.

His mother's soothing voice.

Eufeeling.

It had been with him then, often. Later, less. Then, lost.

Do we know Eufeeling in our innocence, only to lose it with our innocence?

"I have it now," he thought. "I couldn't let go if I tried."

Eufeeling was always there, just beyond thought. All he had to do was turn his awareness toward it — like shining a flashlight — and it leapt into view, bright, luminous. Lighting his life, and somehow lighting others.

It was the steady hum of a hidden machine, the faint music of the spheres. Always present, unnoticed, until he listened. And once he listened, he could not unhear it.

Supporting him whether or not he was aware. Stronger when he was.

He leaned back, fingers loose, heart still. What if children grew up with this? If teachers, parents, leaders lived by it?

The thought shivered through him.

This was no accident of mood. It felt older than him, older than memory. As if humanity itself had once lived by it — and lost it.

A golden age, waiting.

CHAPTER 16

The Feather

The day was warmer than it should have been, as if the sun had forgotten the season. Birds called in bright chorus, ice cracked on the pond like old bones stretching awake.

Ellie felt schoolgirl young, almost giddy. Why?

Ben's kindness? Yes, his support was steady, his tenderness unlike anything she had known. A fondness was blossoming there, loosening old caution.

The Eufeeling group? Also thriving. They accepted her challenge, practicing with friends, family, even pets and a stubborn ficus. Healings were multiplying, mostly successful, always inspiring. Seven new seekers joined last week, more expected today.

Grubner? Never.

No, this was something else — intangible, unknown, waiting.

At the café door she paused, holding it for a woman balancing two trays of coffee. Inside was warm, crowded, cheery. Barb spotted her across the bustle, waving like a flag.

"The usual?" Barb shouted over the din.

Ellie nodded and pointed toward the side room. She slipped through the press of bodies and chose the sunlit table by the window. A long breath escaped her, sunshine filling her chest, Eufeeling rising like a tide.

A moment later Barb bustled in, eyes sparkling, coffee sloshing onto the saucer as she set it down.

"I've got three more people for this week's meeting," she said, then leaned closer with a grin. "One of them is ridiculously charming."

Ellie laughed, wagging a finger. "Patience, Barb. Wait and watch — emphasis on wait."

"Anyway," Ellie went on, "Ben will guide the newcomers through the Eufeeling Technique."

"And you?" Barb asked, brow furrowed.

Ellie held her gaze. "I'll be there. But I've planned something different for the rest of you. Today, we'll practice Eufeeling healing."

Barb's face lit up even brighter. She hurried off, more excited than when she arrived.

Ellie turned to the window again. She breathed once, twice. First Stillness — sweet, full, joyous. Then the gate opened wider. The warmth swelled, absolute, unyielding, all-permeating.

Her breath caught, her head bowed. The café blurred. Wood floor became warm stone, radiator tick tock gave way to soft dove-coos, still air lifted into a gentle wind. Dream, vision — or something older, truer.

Dometius stood before her — robed, kind-eyed, weighted with the wisdom of ages. But this time he looked not as a teacher, but as one standing in wonder.

"I feel it," he said, voice trembling, "Wonderous. In my time… my work… it called me sometimes, touched me lightly. You inhale it with your every breath."

Ellie's breath quivered. The bliss untold. Benevolence. A flower of a thousand petals.

"It's Stillness," she murmured.

Dometius met her gaze. "Yes. But something more. Feel how it moves you. Its life… your life. It lives through you now — as love itself.

It came kindly to her lips. The sound faintly formed. "Eufeeling," she whispered.

His eyes moistened. "So that is its name."

Eufeeling blossomed between them — he had known the touch of Stillness, she, its fullness. Their every cell now bathed in its presence.

Dometius bowed his head. "Then my work is done."

The light shifted. Stone shimmered into wood; dove-song faded to the low hum of conversation. The scent of coffee replaced the wind of memory.

On the table before her lay a single white feather — delicate, luminous, impossibly real. The vision had dissolved, but the sign remained.

She stared, heart thudding, then lifted it carefully, holding it upright as though it were a living thing. In the sunlight it glowed translucent, unbreakable. Stillness moved through her again — only now she spoke its name. *Eufeeling.*

She pressed the feather to her heart. Whatever this presence was — this gentle current of creation — she would live it, and let it live through her.

CHAPTER 17

Sat Yuga

Cold blackness. Bottomless night. Hours before Vigils.

Dometius lay unsleeping. Seething. Villagers' cries breaching the gates. Piercing stone. Piercing hearts.

They did not ask for bread. They asked for silence. Silence that heals.

He ached to go. But the elders forbade it. The elders whisper of disgrace. Yet Dometius sees their doubt — and their yearning.

He rises. Sandals. Beads tangled in hand. Moves into the dark. Toward the gates.

For days, he and a clutch of younger monks walked among the villagers. Sharing Eufeeling. Healing wounds. Lifting spirits. Soul to soul.

At first, the people were wary. Whispered behind doors. But whispers grew into reverence. They welcomed the monks into hearth and home.

Two novices laid down their vows. The village became their monastery.

"They are sent by merciful gods," some said. Others: "They are gods."

But the monks were untouched by vanity or greed. Eufeeling was their bread. Their robe. Their rest.

Despite pressure, Dometius held to his cloister duties. Extra tasks. Unfair rebukes. Still he endured.

One night, leaving the rectory, walking the cloister path— A voice slid from the shadows.

"Brother Dometius."

The Archimandrite. Overseer of seven monasteries. Robes immaculate. Jeweled cross glinting. Smile sharp as a knife.

"I am told the villagers gather again. At your gate."

"They come seeking silence," Dometius said. "They find in it a balm."

The Archimandrite drew closer, voice low though none were near. "Perhaps a balm. Or perhaps an exhibition. Do you not see how our order is diminished? Beggars limping through our courts as if it were a bazaar?"

"They ask not for coin," Dometius replied. "Only to rest where the Spirit rests."

"Words," the Archimandrite murmured, "are easy when one bears no burden of governance. I must answer to men who weigh reputation like gold. And what shall I tell them, when silence itself is turned to talisman?"

The air soured. Dometius felt the weight of the man's intent, pressing his chest.

"I warn you, brother," the Archimandrite whispered, venom sweet. "If you persist, you will find not all your brethren share your charity. Some whisper already of arrogance. Of pride."

Pride. A monk's bane. Poison enough to undo him.

Dometius bowed his head, not in submission but in prayer. "If pride finds me, may God strip me bare. Until then, I will not turn away the ones who come."

The Archimandrite's smile widened. His eyes remained cold. "Then may God grant you wisdom, Brother. You will need it."

He turned, robes trailing like serpents across stone.

Life changed. The vow of silence pressed upon him. His workload tripled. No time beyond the walls. Fewer villagers came to the gates. Then none.

Dometius burned with grief. To heal was forbidden. To remain silent—commanded. The young monks he had trained slipped away. Their fate unknown.

At last the vow lifted. He hurried to the village. Sandals biting dust. What he found stunned him.

Streets clean. Children radiant. No beggars. No hunger.

New houses rose. Old ones mended. A hall with a tall steeple. Bell tolling noon. The square alive — tents, carts, bright fabrics from distant lands. Traders drawn to a people known for honesty.

But greater still were the villagers themselves. Bright-eyed. Virtuous. Free. No jail. No need.

Two novices—once his pupils, now villagers—ran to him with open arms. Exuberant, laughing, flinging words like scattering birds. They led him to a small home, built in ten days with the village's hands.

"This room, Brother, is for you. Come when you wish. Or always."

Over tea and dates they told the story.

At first hard. Suffering. Work.

Then less suffering, more work.

Then work became play.

Now — work is play.

"How was this done?" Dometius asked, heart racing.

"We offered silence. They accepted. We healed, they fed. Soon even without us, villagers reflected the silence. One, then many. Now the whole village lives by the Nothing."

Dometius pressed them. "But so quickly? How can this be?"

They answered with a smile. "Like boiling water. First small currents. Then bubbles. Then the pot roils over."

That night, back at the cloister, lamp sputtering — Dometius unrolled the Vedas. The Yugas. Ages of light and darkness.

His hand stilled at Sat Yuga. The Age of Awakening. An age of harmony. Abundance. Peace.

Could it begin with one heart, utterly still? For a moment — could it be me?

The thought flickered. Faded. He wrote in the margin: Someday, perhaps, another will read this.

Ellie. Eyes closed. Lamp flickering. Papers stirring in a breeze not there. Walls breathing.

The ripples had begun. And they would not be called back.

📖 Reflection: The Yuga Within

Dometius wondered if Sat Yuga — the Age of Awakening — could begin in a single soul.

So can you.

Close your eyes.

Notice the silence between thoughts.

Rest there, if only for a breath.

Ask nothing.

See what is offered.

Ellie's reminder: "Perhaps Sat Yuga doesn't wait for the stars, but for us."

CHAPTER 18

Doubt

A cold rain slashed window. Soaking shoes, umbrellas bent against the wind. Bulging black clouds elbow for a look.

Ellie sat at her desk, reviewing field reports on migration rituals — dry ink, brittle paper, bones of an older world.

A movement in the glass. A man she knew from Acquisitions leaned against her office wall. His hand flattened on the pane, pale, clammy. Head bowed, he swayed unsteadily.

Ellie rushed around her desk, catching his shoulder. "Are you all right?"

"I think so," he muttered, voice thin. "Blood sugar… maybe."

His skin cold. Damp. She touched his forehead, then let go — turned inward. To Eufeeling.

The man steadied. Breath evened. Color returned. Sweat drying.

Relief crossed his face. Then confusion. Then fear.

He jerked back as if her touch burned. "What did you do? Was that voodoo?" His voice rising. "You have no right!" He pulled away, retreating fast, vanishing down the hall.

Ellie stood stunned. Humiliated. A flush of shame and anger. *What just happened? Could Eufeeling harm? Was that even possible? *

That evening, the Eufeeling group gathered — warmth against the chill still lodged in her chest.

Ben stood at the front, teaching the Eufeeling Technique to a full room. His eyes moved gently across the students, noting signs of strain — furrowed brows, darting eyes, restless limbs.

A woman in the second row, dark-red hair, tortoiseshell glasses — she kept opening her eyes, scanning suspiciously, then closing them again. A man in a gray wool suit sat stiff, arms crossed, briefcase at his feet. The rest softened into repose.

When Ben finished, he asked lightly, "Was it easy? Did you notice relaxation, a sense of well-being?"

"No!" the woman blurted, her voice sharp. She glanced around, lips pressed thin. "This is wrong. Against nature.

Heathen work!" Her words choked off. She grabbed her coat and purse, leaving without touching anyone.

Ben turned to the man in the suit. He waited.

"This is Nothing," the man sneered. "A waste of time."

"Did you feel any relaxation? Any ease?" Ben asked softly.

"No!" The man sliced the air with his hand. "I tried to clear my mind. I pushed. I fought. My thoughts never stopped. No peace, no silence. Only frustration!"

"You see —" Ben began.

But the man stood abruptly, voice cracking. "It's all a fraud." He seized his briefcase and stormed after the woman.

Later. Home. Socrates heavy across her lap. Ellie murmured, replaying the day's rejections.

The cat lifted his head, meeting her anxious eyes. A rumbling purr, soft against her hand. "Thanks, Socrates. You understand."

A knock. Quiet. Unexpected.

Ellie peered through the door glass. Ben.

She opened it. "Ben?"

"Hi, Ellie. I hope I'm not intruding. I wanted to check... are you all right?"

"What do you mean?" she asked, though she knew.

"The group tonight. You seemed unsettled. Even Frank was worried."

"Yes," she admitted. "I am. Come in."

They stood by the sofa. Waiting.

"This morning," Ellie whispered, eyes lowered, "a man from Acquisitions collapsed outside my office. I helped him — or thought I did. He recovered but looked at me like I was poison."

Her throat tightened. "And tonight, the woman, the man… they called it wrong. Heathen. Fraud. Angry."

Her voice cracked. "Is Eufeeling hurtful, Ben? Could it be dangerous?" Tears blurred her vision.

Ben gathered her into his arms. She pressed against him, sobbing into his shirt.

"Ellie," he said firmly, holding her shoulders, "not everyone is ready. That doesn't make it false."

"But what if it hurts?"

"It can't," he said gently. "But fear can."

Elsewhere, the faint whirr of a copier. Fingernails on a keyboard. The stale hum of fluorescent lights outside Dr. Grubner's office.

Dr. Robert Kilner, Vice Director of the Museum, strode in. He leaned across Grubner's desk, both hands planted, face close.

"Gill," he said with iron in his tone, "this is getting out of hand. She is a distraction. An embarrassment. Benefactors are asking questions. And I answer to President Tillerman. He is not pleased."

"Yes, sir," Grubner stammered, mouth dry. "I've already addressed it. She won't be a problem."

"When?" Kilner snapped.

"Wednesday morning," Grubner said, voice trembling, then steadier. "I confronted her. In front of Anandamaya and Rashid from the Indian delegation. And Whitehead. They all heard. She was warned."

"This is Friday." Kilner spat the words, a spray hitting the desk. "And she's still at it. Fix it!"

At that same hour, Ellie sat in the archives. Dust motes rising. A brittle parchment spread across her lap.

Halfway down, the hand of Dometius — steady, measured. Then, slashed across it in heavy strokes, another hand:

Beware the pride of false healers. What seems holy may shame the order. Silence twisted is no silence at all.

Ellie traced the gouged fibers, heart pounding. Not correction, but condemnation. A scar across centuries.

Her chest tightened. She heard the sneer in those strokes, the same tone she'd faced in professors and in the field, now reaching through time to accuse her too.

Had Ben been wrong? Was Stillness dangerous?

Her eyes drifted to the feather on her desk. White. Weightless. Pure.

She brushed it along her cheek, grounding herself in its softness.

"No," she whispered. "Not pride. Not spectacle. The gift is real."

The doubt erased. Yet the Archimandrite's shadow lingered, pressed deep into the page.

CHAPTER 19

Healing with Eufeeling

Ben's voice slowed into silence, words falling away until only the hush remained. The newcomers sat quietly, faces softening, a brightness behind their eyes as the silence deepened. When the practice ended, there was a hush in the room. Ellie felt a rush of pride. He had carried it well.

Now it was her turn. She stepped into the center, motioning for Barb.

"Let's do this standing," Ellie said. "So, everyone can see. Because Eufeeling isn't tied to a chair or cushion or special posture. It can happen anywhere — in a café, in the kitchen, in a waiting room. Anytime, anywhere."

Barb joined her, shifting nervously. Ellie smiled reassuringly.

"Here's all you need to do, Barb. Let your mind wander. Don't try to focus, don't try to relax. Just let your thoughts go where they will — that's all."

Barb nodded, a little uncertain but willing.

Ellie closed her eyes. She laid her hand softly on Barb's shoulder. She didn't imagine energy flowing, or picture Barb changing. She simply let Eufeeling rise within her — that effortless fullness. That was all.

The room stilled. Barb's shoulders softened, her face smoothed as if years had slipped away. Her breathing grew quiet, then paused altogether, chest resting in stillness. After a moment, her body began to sway gently, as though rocked by an invisible tide.

A murmur rippled through the circle. Some leaned forward, whispering. Ellie opened her eyes. No need for closed eyes. Eufeeling was full. She saw — the loosened muscles, the quiet breath, the subtle sheen of warmth on Barb's forehead. She had seen it before. The signs were always different, yet always the same.

After a minute, Ellie lifted her voice softly: "Do you see? I'm not sending her energy. I'm not trying to make something happen. I'm only experiencing Eufeeling — with her. No energy is sent. Nothing passes between us. Eufeeling itself is enough."

Barb's swaying slowed. Her eyes blinked open, damp and shining. "I felt… light. As if I wasn't standing on the floor at all but being carried. And something in me — something heavy — just let go."

Ellie nodded gently. "That's the beauty of it. Healing arises naturally. Not because I did anything, but because

Eufeeling was here. Barb experienced it in the way she needed. And I received something too — my chest feels lighter."

The group sat silent, absorbing the moment.

"Now it's your turn," Ellie said. "Pair up. Stand facing each other. Nothing formal. Just as you are."

Chairs scraped, laughter rose nervously, but soon everyone was paired. Ellie raised her hand for quiet.

"Remember — you don't do this for your partner. You don't push, you don't send, you don't fix. You simply rest in Eufeeling, with them. That's all."

"Now, quietly remind your partner to let their mind wander, make gentle contact…then Eufeeling."

The room settled. Eyes closed.

Ellie moved quietly among them. She saw shoulders relax, arms grow loose, spines soften. One pair began to sway together, unplanned, like trees leaning with the same breeze. Another partner's face slackened into an unexpected smile. A grey-haired woman began to weep, not from sorrow but release.

"I don't know why I'm crying," she whispered to her partner. "But it feels good."

Ellie touched her shoulder lightly. "Let it be. That's Eufeeling finding its own way."

Across the circle, Barb whispered, "Look — his breathing!" Everyone turned to see a man standing utterly still, chest relaxed, unmoving, serene.

The silence deepened until it filled the air. Not just the partners — the entire circle was caught in the current, sharing the same expanded, noiseless rhythm.

After a time Ellie said, "Gently break contact with your partner. Open your eyes when you're ready."

Eyes blinked open, smiles flickered, hands rubbed at arms or chests as though rediscovering themselves.

"I felt warmth flood right through me," one man said, surprised. "Like sunlight on water. And I wasn't trying at all."

Ellie smiled. "Yes. That's the heart of it. You rest in Eufeeling. You don't do. You don't intend. Healing happens — naturally, uniquely, perfectly."

The group lingered, reluctant to break the silence. Ellie glanced at the feather on the windowsill, its vane shimmering in the fading light. It stirred, then slowly lifted, rising as if on a faint convection current — perhaps the radiator, perhaps the day's last warmth still trapped in the glass. Drifting toward her, it hovered for a breath. Ellie raised her hand. The feather settled in her palm, weightless.

The feather trembled in her hand.

Dometius' words returned: Stillness is the kingdom.

The ripples were widening. She could feel them now — moving through Ben, through Barb, through every soul in the room. And they would spread further still.

📖 Practice: Healing with Eufeeling

Ellie taught her circle that healing in Eufeeling is not about doing anything *to* another person. It is resting together in Eufeeling and allowing healing to unfold on its own. You can try it now.

1. Initiator: Stand near and gently touch your partner. No ritual needed.

2. Partner's role: Let the mind wander anywhere it wants. No effort, no focus.

3. Initiator's role: Become aware of Eufeeling. Do not send energy, imagine results, or try to heal.

4. Stand together: Simply rest in Eufeeling, with them. Healing unfolds on its own.

5. Notice: Swaying, softened muscles, refined breathing, warmth — these may appear naturally.

❖ Optional

- For physical or emotional concerns: your partner can quietly "grade" discomfort before and after (0 = none, 10 = maximum). Often, the shift is plain.

- For emotional concerns: No need to share emotional concerns with initiator. Eufeeling knows what to do.

○ A parable

Imagine stepping into warm mineral springs with a headache or worry. After a while, both ease. Another person slips into the water with high blood pressure or anger at his boss — he floats awhile, and both dissolve. Did you heal him? No — the waters did.

In the same way, healing in Eufeeling is not *from* you, but in the Eufeeling you share.

Ellie's reminder: "You don't do this for someone. You do it with them. Healing happens on its own."

❏ Deeper background: *The Secret of Instant Healing* by Frank Kinslow

CHAPTER 20

Whispers

Rain traced the museum's glass walls, each line a whispering thread. Corridors echoed with footsteps and low voices. When Ellie passed, conversations stilled. A glance over a shoulder, a murmur cut short. The air thick with things unsaid.

She quickened her pace, clutching her notebook. The knot in her stomach tightened.

What did they know? The manuscripts? Grubner's warning flashed — sharp, waiting for her to slip.

In his office, Dr. Grubner sat stiffly behind his desk. Across from him leaned Dr. Robert Kilner, second visit, eyes hard, nostrils flared. Wind rattled the windowpane.

"The benefactors are uneasy," Kilner said. "What exactly is she doing? What are people seeing in those rooms?"

"Wren is overzealous," Grubner managed. "I made it clear this time. She won't be a distraction."

"Not enough." Kilner's hand struck the desk, rattling a pen. "Our patrons expect order. Fix it."

Later, in the break room, Tiffany found Ellie staring into her coffee.

"Hey," Tiffany said lightly, "don't let them get to you. People whisper when they don't understand. Give them time."

Ellie tried to smile. "Time… I don't know if I have that."

"They'll come around," Tiffany insisted. "You'll see."

That night, the feather lay across Ellie's notes. Lamplight caught its edge, casting a delicate shadow. Instead of comfort, she felt echoes — glances, whispers, distrust. Even the feather seemed subdued, its whiteness dulled by doubt.

She closed her eyes. The silence started. Even silence can be twisted into suspicion. It retreated.

Nothing worked. She gave in. Stopped trying.

Stillness was waiting.

Her wounds began to heal. Ellie lifted the feather. Essence of flight. Freedom.

She turned to Eufeeling, the final embrace — the living expression of Stillness.

Freedom — not escape, but arrival. Absolute. Unshaken. Yes.

CHAPTER 21

Living Eufeeling

The city had not changed. Taxis grumbled at lights, pigeons scattered in drizzle, an old man wrestled an umbrella. Yet Ellie moved as if through another world.

Eufeeling breathed in everything. Not apart. Not above. *Within.*

Each raindrop struck pavement in perfect cadence. Even traffic carried a hidden pulse. What once pressed on her now passed through her, like wind through light.

Inside the museum, Tiffany hurried down the hall, arms full of folders. She almost dropped them when she caught Ellie's gaze. Something in that look slowed her. The weight seemed lighter, breath steadier. She blinked, puzzled, then smiled — as if quietly reassured without a word.

Ellie smiled back. She had not given comfort. She had rested in what was already there. Eufeeling moved where it willed.

113

That evening, at home, Socrates sprawled across her lap. His purr vibrated through her legs, deep and resonant. For a moment the room itself purred — lamp, books, silence. Nothing separate. Cat and woman and quiet air: the same unbroken thread.

Later, the circle gathered. Ben guided newcomers gently. Ellie sat in back, hands on knees. She only *was.*

A woman in front struggled, face drawn with effort. Then shoulders softened, brow cleared. She opened her eyes, surprised at her own ease. Ellie had not moved. Eufeeling had spoken.

Ben glanced over, caught in the hush. His voice faltered for half a breath. He looked down quickly, eyes shining with a flicker — not in Ellie, *through* her.

Ellie closed her eyes again. The world did not vanish. It blossomed. If danger came, she would answer. If comfort was needed, she would give it. Not from fear. Not from calculation. But because the moment itself asked.

Eufeeling was not apart from life. It was life — whole, unshaken, free.

📖 Reflection

Look down at the floor. Now quickly look up at the ceiling.

For a split second — *Nothing.*

That Nothing has always been there.

Later, you may glimpse what lies beyond.

— *She taught simply, but inside she knew she was midwifing the same current Dometius had tended: gate, kingdom, and the blooming beyond.*

CHAPTER 22

Dometius Returns

Stone walls pressed close around Dometius. He had grown used to their weight and to the elders' silence. Yet even here he felt the pull of the village beyond — warmth he was forbidden to touch.

The door creaked. Brother Markos slipped inside, breath fast, eyes wide.

"Brother Dometius, Marta's child is failing. We each sat with her, one by one, offering stillness… but she grows weaker."

Dometius closed his eyes. He saw the girl pale on her mat, her mother's trembling hand. His heart ached to go — but the elders' decree was iron.

"Then we shall sit here," he said.

"Here? The girl is far away."

"Stillness is not bound by distance," Dometius said, placing his palm on the stone floor. "What is touched here may be felt there. Sit."

They folded to the floor. No words. No ritual. Only bodies settling, the gentle lowering into silence.

Presence deepened, spreading outward like water through unseen channels. Dometius felt the girl's breath falter, then steady — though she was nowhere near. He did not move, only rested in the current until dawn paled the cell.

At first light, Markos slipped away. Hours later he returned, eyes alight.

"She is well," he whispered. "Her fever broke in the night. Her mother says… it began just when we sat."

That night, by lamplight, Dometius set quill to parchment. *Even across walls, silence finds its way. What is touched in one heart may awaken in another.*

From the rafters, a feather loosened and drifted down, dark as ink. He regarded it quietly — not omen, not blessing. Only reminder. He dipped the quill and added: *When silence is shared, healing multiplies. Stillness wears many colors. *

📖 Practice: Remote Healing

Dometius discovered that Stillness is not bound by walls. You can notice this too.

Agree on a time to begin and end.

Partner's role: Sit comfortably (or lie down if unwell). Let the mind wander freely. No focus, no effort.

Initiator's role: Become aware of Eufeeling. Rest in it — no sending, no imagining.

Together: Remain for the agreed time. Initiator resting in Eufeeling. Partner mind wandering as it will.

Notice afterward: Healing may unfold uniquely for each — quietly, naturally.

❖ Dometius' reminder: "Even across walls, silence finds its way. What is touched in one heart may awaken in another."

❏ Deeper background: *The Secret of Instant Healing* by Frank Kinslow

CHAPTER 23

The Rift

The circle filled the rented hall, folding chairs scraping as people settled. Most leaned forward, eyes bright with curiosity. A few shifted uneasily, new faces testing the waters.

Ben guided the newcomers gently into the Eufeeling Technique. Silence lingered, light but steady. Then voices began to stir.

"I... I don't know," a woman near the door whispered, trembling. "It feels too strong. I don't know if I can bear it. My chest — grief — like it will break me." She buried her face in her hands.

Ellie rose slowly, her presence quieting the shuffle of chairs. She moved to the woman, knelt beside her, and laid a hand softly over hers.

"You don't have to bear it," Ellie said gently. "Let it be here. Let it move as it will. You don't need to fix it. Just rest in Eufeeling with it."

The woman's shoulders shook, then softened. Her breath steadied. Tears flowed, but lighter now, like a stream freed of stone.

Ellie lifted her head, her voice carrying to the group:

"Emotions are not enemies. They are visitors. When we rest in Eufeeling, we don't chase them away or clutch them close. We let them be. And in that allowance, they heal themselves."

Tiffany shot her hand into the air, eyes wide. "So we don't fight our feelings?"

Ellie smiled. "No fight. No fear. Only Eufeeling — within the sorrow, within the fear. Nothing is excluded."

A hush settled. Then a man, new to the group, in work clothes, hands scarred and rough, spoke hesitantly:

"My wife hasn't slept a full night in months. Last night she did. I don't know why, but… she smiled this morning, like she used to." His eyes brimmed. "If this is what you call Eufeeling, I want to know more."

Across the room, a young woman clutched a photograph of her children. She raised it slightly, voice wavering. "I tried what you showed us last week. Just a few minutes, sitting in their room while they slept. The fighting between them stopped. Yesterday they played together again." She looked down, shaking her head in wonder. "I didn't tell them a word."

The testimonies rippled outward, one voice sparking another. Small, ordinary lives — yet touched by something larger than themselves. The circle leaned in, knit together by the invisible thread of what they had all felt.

Toward the back, a newcomer sat stiff, arms folded, gaze unreadable. He had not joined the practice, only watched. At intervals, he scribbled in a small notebook, his eyes flicking now and again toward Ellie. She noticed but said nothing.

The group exhaled together. The rift had not torn them apart. Instead, it had revealed strength — the circle more whole than before. Still, in the shadow of the spy's pen, another ripple was forming.

CHAPTER 24

Wider Ripples

Night again. The city outside hummed with its familiar clatter — horns, engines, hurried footsteps. Yet in Ellie's small apartment the air shimmered, as though listening.

She had stopped trying to force Eufeeling. Now it simply was. Within her, around her, even in the silence between refrigerator clicks. She sat at her desk, the white feather resting across her journal.

Her eyelids grew heavy. The lamplight blurred, shadows softening into something older, truer.

Stone beneath her feet. Warm air carrying the scent of olive and pine. Ahead stood Dometius, his robe brushing the ground. In his hand he held a single black feather, its edge sharp against the glow.

He lifted it slightly. Ellie looked down at her palm — the white feather was there. Light meeting dark.

Dometius' gaze was steady, kind. He said nothing. The silence between them widened, alive. Not a gulf, not a barrier — a bridge.

Then, as if carried by the same unseen breath, both feathers stirred. Lifted. Floated. For a heartbeat they touched in the air, brushing vane to vane.

Ellie's chest swelled. She felt the pulse of something beyond either of them — a current moving outward, past cloister and café, past centuries. Wider ripples.

Her eyes blinked open. She was back in her room. The feather lay unmoved across her journal. Yet the air still carried the slight scent of pine. And that hush.

Ellie whispered, "So this is what happens when we stop holding back. The ripples spread. Not mine. Not his. Just the current itself."

The feather trembled faintly, then stilled.

📖 Practice: Inner-Outer

Ellie realized that release doesn't come from trying to relax, but from letting Eufeeling fill and expand. You can try it now.

Step 1. Sit comfortably

Close your eyes.

Step 2. Become aware of Eufeeling

Let Eufeeling rise in your awareness — light, effortless.

Step 3. Sense your whole body in that Eufeeling

Notice your body as a whole, at the same time as Eufeeling.

Step 4. Let Eufeeling expand

Allow Eufeeling to spread naturally beyond your body — filling the space around you, the whole room.

Step 5. Rest in the widening

No effort, no control. Just notice how the body savors the gentle fullness of Eufeeling.

Ellie's reminder: "You don't release tension by trying. You release it by letting Eufeeling grow larger than the body that holds it."

❏ Deeper background: *Awefeeling; How You Can Decrease Pain, Break Negative Patterns, and Find Peace in Only 31/2 Minutes a Day* by Frank Kinslow

CHAPTER 25

The Archimandrite's Hand

The cloister bell tolled compline, the air heavy with incense and fading light. Dometius walked slowly along the inner path, beads tangled in his fingers. His sandals scraped stone worn by centuries of prayer.

A rustle of robes. The Archimandrite emerged from the shadows, flanked by two elders. His jeweled cross caught the last flame of sun, throwing a shard of light across the courtyard.

"Brother Dometius," he said softly, the kind of softness sharpened with threat. "You persist. Villagers gather. Novices slip from their vows. And worse — your hand scratches words onto parchment, dangerous words."

He gestured. One elder unrolled a sheet, Dometius' careful script now marred by heavy black lines in another's hand. Beware the pride of false healers.

"Your writings spread doubt," the Archimandrite continued. "This… corruption must end. If you will not surrender them, we will take them. And you will be removed from this order. Cast out. A beggar among beggars."

The words struck like hammer blows. For a moment, silence stretched between them, broken only by the call of a crow echoing from distant white cliffs.

Dometius lifted his gaze. "God alone will judge me; may He strip me bare if pride takes seat. But these words are not mine alone. They belong to whoever needs them, now or centuries hence. They will not be lost."

The Archimandrite's face darkened. He turned sharply, Furious robes. Fleeing sand. The elders followed, their steps echoing long after they were gone.

Dometius stood unmoving. At his feet lay a single black feather, stirred by the evening wind. He bent, lifted it gently, and held it in his palm.

He whispered, "If I cannot guard them openly, I will guard them in silence."

That night, by flickering lamplight, he wrapped the parchments in cloth, sealed them with wax, and carried them down a narrow stair to the oldest part of the cloister. Beneath loose stones, in a hollow cut long before his time, he hid them.

His fingers lingered on the cool rock. "Someday," he murmured, "another will read. Another will carry this forward."

The stones settled into place. The feather rested across the crack like a watchful sentinel.

CHAPTER 26

The Breakthrough

The apartment was still. Even Socrates slept soundly, his paws twitching in dream. Ellie sat alone at her desk, the white feather resting beside her hand.

She closed her eyes. Not to escape. Not to seek. Only to rest.

Silence deepened, effortless. The day's noise, the whispers, the doubts — gone. Even her thoughts were like distant birds, circling but never landing.

Then, in the hush, something opened.

Not just quiet. Not just Eufeeling. But vastness without boundary. Stillness, alive, melding her and the world together.

She felt herself dissolve, not into nothingness but into everything. Each sound — the faint hum of the refrigerator, the distant traffic — was not separate. It was her. She was not hearing it. She was it.

And then — awe.

Not the awe of standing before a mountain or staring into a star-filled sky. This was awe without object. Pure astonishment at existence itself. A wonder so complete it filled her to overflowing until there was no "her" left to overflow.

Ellie opened her eyes. The room looked the same: lamp, books, cat, feather. Yet everything shone as if lit from within.

She whispered, "This is it. Not mine. Not theirs. Just life, awake in itself."

Socrates stretched, blinked up at her, and purred. Ellie laughed softly, tears brimming. Even her cat was woven of Stillness. Even her tears. Even the air between them.

She pressed the feather to her chest. Not for luck. Not for memory. But because it was simply the same as her heartbeat.

Ellie breathed, and the breath had no edge.

Awe.

Eufeeling's secret. Hidden ripples. Cosmic symphony in a doorknob.

Ellie giggled.

📖 Reflection

Sometimes awe comes as thunder — mountains, oceans, stars.

Sometimes it comes as silence without object.

When it does, let it come.

It needs no name, no effort.

It is the world recognizing itself.

❏ Deeper background: *Awefeeling; How You Can Decrease Pain, Break Negative Patterns, and Find Peace in Only 31/2 Minutes a Day* by Frank Kinslow

CHAPTER 27

Betrayal

The museum corridors were hushed, but not with reverence. Hushed like a room after harsh words. Eyes flicked sideways, whispers darted behind cupped hands. Ellie walked through it all, notebook in hand, steady but watchful.

At the far end of the hall, Dr. Grubner spoke with a young man Ellie didn't recognize. Thin, pale, a little too eager in his nods. When he glanced up, his eyes caught hers, then darted quickly away.

Later that evening, Ben arrived at her apartment, his face taut. "They twisted your words," he said. "Someone in the group — they repeated what you said about Eufeeling, but out of context. By the time it reached Grubner, it sounded like you claimed to heal by your own power."

Ellie sat back, the words heavy but strangely hollow. Like echoes that had lost their source.

Ben leaned forward. "This isn't a small thing. They're calling it arrogance. Heresy even. They're saying you've set yourself up above medicine, above God."

Ellie looked at him gently. "Ben… what do you feel right now?"

He blinked, taken aback. "Angry. Protective. Afraid for you."

She nodded, her eyes soft. "That's the ripple. That's their intent. But look closer."

He exhaled slowly. The fear ebbed. Beneath it, something steadier rose — the Eufeeling he had practiced so often. His shoulders lowered. His jaw unclenched.

Ellie smiled. "See? Their words can wound only if we take them in. Stillness holds. It cannot be betrayed."

Outside, the city throbbed — sirens, horns, footsteps. Inside, the silence thickened, not fragile but unbreakable.

At that same hour, Grubner sat in his office. The spy leaned close, recounting what he had seen and heard. Grubner's lips tightened into a smile thin as shaved steel. "Good. We will put her in her place. Once and for all."

He scribbled notes, already planning. "Prepare a report. I'll send it to Dr. Kilner — and perhaps even to our colleagues abroad. If we bury her work deep enough, no one will ever dig it up."

CHAPTER 28

Widening Circles

The circle had outgrown the café's back room. Tonight they met in the community hall, chairs borrowed from every corner, the air buzzing with quiet expectancy. Ellie looked out over the crowd — not just the familiar faces but strangers too, brought by word of mouth, by curiosity, by something they couldn't name.

Ben opened as always, guiding the newcomers gently. His voice was calm, his hands steady. But the air in the room felt different now. Less like a class, more like a gathering tide.

Ellie watched Tiffany lean toward a shy woman at her side, whispering encouragement. Barb — bustling, eager — passed out cups of tea, pressing each one into waiting hands as if it were an offering. Even Frank, quiet in the back row, seemed to glow with a new steadiness, his once-nervous posture now open, unshaken.

Ellie stepped forward. She didn't speak at first. She didn't need to. The silence itself settled like a gentle cloak. When she finally raised her voice, it was almost a whisper, yet everyone heard:

"Eufeeling does not stop with us. It moves outward. Into your families, your neighbors, the people you pass on the street. You don't have to carry it. You don't have to convince anyone. Just rest in it, and it will spread."

She let her eyes wander across the room. A man in a mechanic's jacket. A mother with her child on her lap. A professor she vaguely recognized from another department. Each seemed to soften under her gaze — not by persuasion, but by the Stillness moving through her.

As they practiced, pairs swayed gently, shoulders softened, breaths refined. One man's laughter bubbled up unexpectedly, infectious as it spread. Another began to weep quietly, the woman beside him simply resting a hand on his arm, sharing silence without words.

When it ended, no one hurried to leave. They lingered, reluctant to break the spell. Outside, the rain had stopped, and people walked into the night with lighter steps, as though they carried something invisible yet unmistakable.

Ellie gathered her notes, though she hadn't used them. The feather lay tucked inside, its vane gleaming faintly in the hall's dim light. She pressed the notebook closed, smiling.

The ripples were widening. Not because she pushed them outward, but because the world itself was ready.

📖 Reflection

Eufeeling does not end where you sit.

It moves, quietly, through the people you meet, through voices and silences you never hear.

You do not need to carry it. It is already there.

You only rest in it.

CHAPTER 29

Dometius' Final Page

The years had pressed lines into Dometius' face, but his eyes still carried the same clear flame. From the monastery walls he watched the village below. Children ran through clean streets. Merchants haggled cheerfully in the square. Families shared laughter where once there had been only hunger.

He smiled. They no longer needed him.

The young monks he had taught now walked among the villagers with ease, offering silence as naturally as breath. Healing was no longer a miracle — it had become a way of life. The seed had taken root, grown strong, and now flowered without his tending.

That evening, he sat by lamplight. A blank parchment lay before him. The ink trembled faintly in his hand, but his words were steady.

I have seen the power of silence, nearer than breath. I have seen it carry across distance, heal the sick, soften the fearful, awaken the joyful. But it is not mine to keep. It belongs to those yet to come. To the one who will walk further than I dared.

He paused. The crow's black feather, kept all these years, rested on the corner of his desk. He lifted it, turned it slowly in his hand. Once it had fallen as omen, sharp and dark. Now it seemed only a reminder: endings are also beginnings.

He pressed the feather between the pages of his manuscript, sealing it inside. A final mark.

Then he folded the parchment, tied it carefully with cord, and placed it among the others. He touched the stack lightly, as if blessing a child.

No trumpet. No farewell. Only Stillness, filling the room, the lamp, the night.

When the flame guttered and died, he did not stir to relight it. He had written enough. The rest would be silence.

The Unmasking of Grubner

The boardroom was too warm, its long mahogany table polished to a false shine. Donors sat stiff-backed in their chairs, coats draped neatly, eyes narrowed with expectation. At the head sat Dr. Robert Kilner, jaw set, fingers drumming on the arm of his chair.

Grubner rose, papers quivering in his hands, his voice struggled for authority.

"Colleagues," he began, "I bring you troubling news. Dr. Wren's… gatherings have grown beyond their remit. What began as scholarly exploration has strayed into spectacle — claims of healing, even whispers of powers that defy science. This undermines our institution, our benefactors, our reputation."

A murmur rippled down the table. Ellie sat quietly at the far end, notebook closed, hands resting lightly on its cover. She did not speak.

Grubner's words grew sharper, fueled by the silence. "She deceives. She claims authority not hers. She leads our staff into dangerous fantasies!" He slapped the papers down, voice rising. "It is arrogance — heresy!"

The donors leaned forward, some frowning, others doubtful. Kilner's gaze shifted from Grubner to Ellie. "Do you deny this?"

Ellie lifted her eyes. She did not defend. She did not argue. She let Stillness rise, filling her chest, the room, the pause.

The air changed. A current unseen but unmistakable stilled the restless shuffling, softened the harsh lines in faces. One donor adjusted her glasses, suddenly unsure of her scowl. Another leaned back, sighing as though a weight had slipped off his shoulders.

Grubner faltered. His words, sharp as knives, now rang hollow. He cleared his throat, tried again, but the force had left him. "She… she manipulates perception," he stammered. "You feel it now — don't you see? This is her trick!"

A feather drifted from the open door — pale, ordinary, perhaps from a pigeon on the ledge. It landed on the polished table before Kilner. The room hushed, every eye drawn to its quiet grace.

Ellie did not move. She had not willed it, had not claimed it. The feather was simply there.

One donor chuckled softly. Another shook her head. The tension broke, not into laughter, but into clarity.

Kilner's jaw tightened. He looked from the feather to Ellie, then back to Grubner. His voice was flat. "Enough. You've embarrassed yourself. And this institution."

Grubner opened his mouth, but nothing came. His papers slid from his hand, scattering useless across the floor.

The meeting adjourned in silence. Donors filed out slowly, some pausing to nod politely to Ellie, their eyes softened.

Ellie gathered her notebook. She had not spoken a word. Stillness had spoken for her.

CHAPTER 31

Dawn of Sat Yuga

The hall was crowded beyond its walls. Chairs lined the aisles, windowsills, even the doorway. Some stood in the back, content to lean against the frame. No one wanted to be turned away.

Ellie sat at the circle's center. Ben to her right, Tiffany to her left, Frank and Barb close behind. Faces ringed around them: familiar, new, doubtful, radiant. A tapestry of humanity, bound not by belief but by presence.

There were no introductions, no instructions. Only Eufeeling, breathing through them all.

It began as a murmur — the quiet sigh of a woman loosening her shoulders, the chuckle of a child at her side. Then it spread: a ripple of relaxation, laughter, tears. A man who had walked in with a cane rested it by his chair, forgotten. A mother and daughter leaned into one another, breathing as though from the same chest.

Ellie opened her eyes. She reached for the feather she had carried all these months. Before she could move, Tiffany's hand touched hers lightly. "May I?" she whispered. Ellie nodded.

With care, Tiffany lifted the feather and placed it in the center of the circle. Its vane caught the lamplight, gleaming white against the worn boards.

No one spoke of symbols, yet all eyes fell upon it. For a moment the room itself seemed to pause, not in emptiness but in fullness — as though the feather did not rest on the floor but within the silence that held them all.

Ben's hand brushed Ellie's. She looked at him and saw the glimmer — not in his eyes, but through them. A glimpse. He smiled, not at her, but at what he too had seen. She felt her chest swell, warmth meeting warmth, a quiet knowing that their paths were joined.

Ellie closed her eyes again. She was not leading, not teaching, not carrying. She was simply resting in what had always been there. And the world answered.

Outside, the soft summer night lay over the city. The traffic still hummed, neon still flickered, but the air carried a quiet different from before. Strangers passed each other on the street with slower steps, softer eyes. Something was stirring.

The age had not yet come.

But its breath was here —

in every pause, in every quiet joy.

Waiting.

Already beginning.

And it begins not elsewhere, not later —

but here, with you.

Notes

Notes

About the Kinslow System Organization

Dr. Kinslow is the originator of the Kinslow System™
and sole teacher of Quantum Entrainment® programs.
He conducts seminars and lectures worldwide. For more
information about the Kinslow System, please contact us at:

Website: www.KinslowSystem.com

E-mail: Info@KinslowSystem.com

Kinslow System Products

Books by Dr. Frank Kinslow

The Secret of Instant Healing

The Secret of Quantum Living

Eufeeling! The Art of Creating Inner Peace and Outer Prosperity

The Kinslow System: Your Path to Proven
Success in Health, Love, and Life

Beyond Happiness: Finding and Fulfilling Your Deepest Desire

How to be Happy Without Even Trying

When Nothing Works Try Doing Nothing: How Learning
to Let Go Will Get You Where You Want to Go

Awefeeling: How You Can Decrease Pain, Break Negative Patterns,
and Find Peace in Only 3½ Minutes a Day

Martina and the Ogre (a QE children's book)

Heal Your World, Heal Our World

Audiobooks

The Secret of Instant Healing

The Secret of Quantum Living

Eufeeling! The Art of Creating Inner Peace and Outer Prosperity

When Nothing Works Try Doing Nothing: How Learning
to Let Go Will Get You Where You Want to Go

Awefeeling: How You Can Decrease Pain, Break Negative Patterns,
and Find Peace in Only 3½ Minutes a Day

Martina and the Ogre (a QE children's book)

More…

Downloads & DVDs & CDs

QE Community Membership

QE Private Healing, Coaching and Workshops

* 9 7 9 8 9 9 9 3 3 4 3 0 0 6 *